THE MYSTERY BEGINS

The girl stared at me, eyes wide. Then . . .

"What did you say?" she asked. In English. With an American accent.

"You're American?" George said, looking surprised. I was startled too. What was an American teenager doing picking pockets in Rome?

At that moment Bess puffed up. "You got her!" she cried. Leaning forward, she rested her hands on her knees while she caught her breath.

"Okay, look," I said to the girl. "I know you've been following us and I know you took my friend's wallet."

"No, I didn't!" the girl protested. "How dare you accuse me!"

I sighed. "I don't want to have to get the police involved, but—"

"No! No police!" she cried, her eyes going ever wider.

NANCY DREW
girl detective®

THE HARDY BOYS
UNDERCOVER BROTHERS®

Available from Aladdin Paperbacks

GIRL DETECTIVE ®

NANCY DREW
AND THE
UNDERCOVER BROTHERS ®

HARDY BOYS
Super Mystery #2

DANGER OVERSEAS

CAROLYN KEENE
and
FRANKLIN W. DIXON

Aladdin Paperbacks
NEW YORK LONDON TORONTO SYDNEY

This book is a work of fiction. Any references to historical events, real people,
or real locales are used fictitiously. Other names, characters, places, and incidents
are the product of the author's imagination, and any resemblance to actual events
or locales or persons, living or dead, is entirely coincidental.

ALADDIN PAPERBACKS

An imprint of Simon & Schuster Children's Publishing Division

1230 Avenue of the Americas, New York, NY 10020

Copyright © 2008 by Simon & Schuster, Inc.

All rights reserved, including the right of reproduction in whole or in part in any form.

NANCY DREW, NANCY DREW: GIRL DETECTIVE, THE HARDY BOYS MYSTERY STORIES,

HARDY BOYS UNDERCOVER BROTHERS, ALADDIN PAPERBACKS, and related logo

are registered trademarks of Simon & Schuster, Inc.

Designed by Karin Paprocki

The text of this book was set in Meridien.

Manufactured in the United States of America

First Aladdin Paperbacks edition May 2008

2 4 6 8 10 9 7 5 3 1

Library of Congress Control Number 2008920169

ISBN-13: 978-1-4169-5777-5

ISBN-10: 1-4169-5777-4

CONTENTS

DANGER OVERSEAS

CHAPTER 1

FRANK

AN AVALANCHE OF TROUBLE

"I'm gonna rip your lungs out and pop them like balloons!"

"You already said that," I reminded the masked wrestler as I ducked under a swinging fist the size of a roast chicken. "Zero points for creativity."

"*Aaaaarrrggghhh!*" he roared, and lunged at me. I guessed he must have run out of snappy one-liners. Unfortunately for me, he hadn't run out of energy. He might be an idiot in a ridiculous outfit of lederhosen and suspenders over a bare chest, but there was easily 250 pounds of him against my 170, and he was trying to squash me.

I jumped back and to the side. As the wrestler lumbered past me I linked my fingers and delivered a quick two-handed kidney chop. Bellowing, he fell forward. His head in its laced leather mask whacked against the wall with a sickeningly loud thud. He hit the floor and stayed down. I winced. That was a concussion for sure.

I contemplated him as he lay there. He was more than 250 pounds, I decided. Maybe even more than three hundred. I shook my head. "Man," I muttered

When Joe and I got this mission from ATAC, no one told us we were going to be facing three-hundred-pound masked wrestlers. I thought it was all about bet-fixing on a college wrestling team. That I'd been prepared for.

Where was Joe, anyway? He'd been keeping watch outside the door to the office where I was downloading files off the computer—or so I thought. But that hadn't stopped Lederhosen Man from walking in on me. Had something happened to my little bro?

My thoughts were interrupted by a door slamming behind me. "You're going down!" a new voice roared.

I spun around—and groaned. Lederhosen Man's evil twin had just arrived. This guy was wearing the same ridiculous outfit, but I wasn't laughing. He was even bigger than the first guy—at least six foot six and massively muscle-bound. The two of them, I remembered now, formed a duo called the Alpine Avalanche.

"Uh—I don't suppose we could just talk about this calmly?" I offered. "Maybe over coffee?"

In answer, the wrestler roared and ran at me, arms outstretched.

I faked to the left, then threw myself to the right and rolled over the top of a low file cabinet. I came up in a crouch on the other side.

Lederhosen Twin number two was a little quicker on the uptake than his fallen brother. He had seen through my fakeout and was facing me. An evil grin spread across his face.

I shoved the file cabinet, which was on wheels, at him. He deflected it easily. But I was already halfway across the room, racing for the door.

"No you don't!" Lederhosen grunted. Moving with surprising speed, he leaped after me and grabbed my left arm. He twisted it behind my back and then hooked his own massive arm through it. "This is called a chicken wing," he said in my ear. I felt a fiery pain as he pulled upward.

"Aaagh!" I yelled.

"And this"—he went to hook his other arm through my other one—"is a double chicken wing."

Before he could complete the move, I drove my elbow as hard as I could into his gut. He grunted and the pressure on my left arm eased for a second. It was all I needed. I twisted free, spun, and landed a chopping blow at the pressure point on his shoulder.

Well, that's what I meant to do, anyway. What

actually happened was that my hand hit what felt like a leather-covered anvil. The guy's shoulder was so heavily muscled that I couldn't even find his pressure point.

He just looked at me and his grin got wider.

I skipped backward as fast as I could. A noise to my right made me glance over. My heart hit my boots. Lederhosen Twin number one was clambering to his feet. And he looked, well, kind of mad.

Uh-oh.

"Joe, a little help?" I called, though I didn't think it would do much good. If Joe were nearby, he'd have been in here by now.

The Lederhosen Twins began to close in on me. "It's avalanche time," the smaller one snarled.

I gulped.

Then I heard a snorting rumble, like a supercharged V-8 engine, outside the door. A second later there was a crash.

The metal door burst inward, blown completely out of the doorframe. Through clouds of plaster dust and debris, a massive black monster truck painted with Day-Glo green flames loomed. The engine revved. What do you know? It *was* a supercharged V-8. The Lederhosen Twins gawked.

The passenger door swung open. "Hop in, Frank!" Joe's voice called. "I got us a ride!"

I laughed out loud as I raced for the open door. I jumped in and slammed it behind me. "I was starting to think you'd bailed on me. Glad you could make it to the party," I told my brother. "Nice wheels."

"Aren't they special?" Grinning, Joe stabbed a button on the dashboard. A monstrously distorted voice rang out from a loudspeaker mounted on the truck's roof.

"I am the GRAVEDIGGER!" it screamed. "Say your prayers while I dig your GRAVE!"

Joe shifted into reverse and backed down the long hallway of the sports complex at full speed. "When I saw the size of those two goons, I figured we'd need more than just our muscles," he explained. "So I, uh, borrowed this."

"It's a stylin' ride." I watched the furious faces of the Lederhosen Twins get smaller and smaller.

"Did you get the files?" Joe asked me, his eyes on the rearview mirror.

I held up a CD in a case. "Right here."

Still in reverse, Joe swerved to the left and we zoomed down a wide ramp and out the open doors of a loading bay. We rolled to a stop across a parking lot from the arena, next to our own car. Joe grinned and we high-fived.

Mission accomplished! Finishing an assignment always gave me a rush.

As we drove toward home, though, I felt some of the excitement drain away. My left shoulder gave a twinge where it had been chicken-winged. I winced and rolled it, trying to work out the soreness.

"Is it just me," I said, "or does it seem like all the missions we're getting from ATAC these days seem to involve bad guys of unusual size?"

"Hmm. Well, there were those biker thugs we had to deal with on the last mission," Joe said in a thoughtful voice.

"And before that we had to investigate that football team for the steroids thing," I added.

Joe shrugged. "What about it?"

"I don't know. I'm just a little sick of getting pounded on by plus-size dudes," I said. I rubbed my sore shoulder some more.

Joe braked at a light and turned to look at me. His blue eyes were narrowed in puzzlement. "What are you saying, bro? You want to quit doing missions for ATAC?"

ATAC stands for American Teens Against Crime. It's a secret organization that was founded by our dad, Fenton Hardy. It's grown into a pretty major thing. We have agents all across the country. Our job is to tackle the things that the ordinary, adult branches of law enforcement can't easily handle—crimes in which teenagers are involved, a lot of it organized crime, but being carried out by people the same age as me or Joe. Sometimes, of course, it leads us to adult criminals, as our last couple of cases had.

It's the coolest thing I've ever done.

"Don't be an idiot," I retorted. I slapped the side of Joe's head just for good measure. "Of course I'd never quit ATAC. I just wouldn't mind a different kind of mission, that's all. You know, where we get to use our brains a little more and our brawn a little less."

"I hear you. James Bond stuff," Joe said. He glanced in the rearview mirror and slicked back his blond hair. "Hardy, Joe Hardy," he said in a terrible fake English accent. Then he grinned. "Hey, as long as we get the hot girls like Bond, I'm all for it."

I snorted. "You have a one track mind, have I told you that lately?"

Things were quiet for a couple of days after that. The local news was full of the arrest of a college wrestling coach in the next town over for a bet-fixing scam. Our aunt Trudy, who lives with us, clucked her tongue as she watched the story on TV one afternoon. "Can you imagine?" she said to no one in particular. "It's a good thing Frank and Joe have never gotten mixed up in anything like that."

"Who, us?" Joe put on his most innocent face.

Aunt Trudy has no idea that Joe and I are in ATAC—or that ATAC even exists, for that matter.

I heard the kitchen door open. Our mom's voice called, "Frank? Joe?"

"In the living room," Joe hollered back.

"Hi, Mom," I added.

"Boys, there's a car full of groceries in the driveway. Would you unload them, please?"

"Sure thing, Mom," I answered, prying myself off the couch. Beside me, Joe hadn't moved. I poked him. "I'm not doing it by myself."

"Slaves. We're slaves in our own house," Joe grumbled as he followed me out to Mom's car.

"Joe?"

"What?"

"Shut up."

I opened the hatch door and started pulling bags out of the back of Mom's SUV. Joe and I each made two trips inside. Then, as I was setting the last of the bags on the kitchen counter, I noticed an ad circular sticking out the top. It was for a local video arcade. On red paper, it was crudely printed and clearly homemade. "TRY ARE LATEST GAME, ATAC OF THE ZOMBOID!" it shouted in big block letters. A CD in a cardboard sleeve was attached.

Atac of the Zomboid? My scalp prickled. That was no random typo. It had to be from ATAC! That's how they sent us our new missions—in innocent-looking packages.

I pulled the flyer out of the bag. But before I could show it to Joe, Aunt Trudy snatched it out of my hands. "What's this?" she demanded. "Atac of the Zomboid? Oh, goodness, and have you ever seen such terrible spelling? These people who work at the arcade ought to be forced to go back to school!" Crumpling the flyer, she made to toss the whole thing into the garbage.

"Aunt Trudy, don't!" I shouted, panicked.

"Don't what?" she said severely. "Don't tell me you actually want to try out this silly game. Frank, it's obvious these computer games are terrible for young people's brains. I'm doing you a favor, I really am." And she threw the disk and the flyer right into the garbage pail—which happened to be full of rotten produce, as Mom had just finished cleaning out the fridge.

Oh, ugh. I stifled a groan. Now I was going to have to get that disk out. . . .

Fortunately Aunt Trudy and Mom had disappeared into the pantry. Taking a deep breath, I reached into the garbage and fished out the CD. A bit of slimy rotten cucumber clung to the cardboard sleeve. I grimaced as I carried it to the sink and rinsed it off.

Joe was grinning at me. "Better you than me," he said in a low voice. "I'm guessing that's not really an arcade game?"

"The things I put up with for ATAC," I said with a sigh. "Come on, let's see what's going on."

Upstairs in my room, I slotted the CD into my computer's disk drive and clicked Play.

A mug shot of a young guy, maybe a year older than me, appeared on my screen. He had shaggy, light brown hair and deep, dark circles under his brown eyes.

"Sam Lewis," a voiceover began. "Age twenty, student of archaeology at Rochester State. Arrested in Rome, Italy, when he tried to sell stolen archaeological artifacts in an online auction." The photo changed to show two small, etched medallions that looked as if they might be made of gold.

"Rome?" Joe commented. "What does that have to do with us? ATAC is an American operation."

I shook my head, baffled. "Let's see."

The next thing that appeared was a grainy video sequence. It showed Sam Lewis being questioned by an Italian police officer. The room they were in looked like the interrogation room of any police station—dingy, with yellowish beige paint on walls that were otherwise bare. The only furniture was a metal table and two metal chairs.

"Who were you working with?" the bearded officer asked in excellent English. "You must have had help."

Sam just shook his head.

"We know you did not steal these objects on your

own," the officer insisted. "Tell us who helped you, or you will have even more trouble than you do now."

Sam gave a short laugh. "That's not possible," he muttered.

"We can help you," the officer said, switching tactics. "If you tell us who you were working with, we can make sure you get a lighter punishment. Why don't you want to help us help you?"

Sam turned away, his lips pressed tightly together. "I can't help you. And you can't help me."

I squinted at the video. Fluorescent lights made harsh shadows on Sam's face, which looked tired and drawn.

"He seems scared of something," Joe commented.

I nodded. That was just what I'd been thinking. "But of what? He's already been caught. Anything he tells them at this point can only make things better, I'd think. What does he have to lose?"

Joe leaned back in his chair and folded his arms. "Maybe whoever helped him steal those artifacts is scarier than the police."

The video froze on a closeup of Sam's face and the voice-over resumed.

"The Italian authorities haven't been able to get Sam to say anything more. We know he must have had some help, because certain records were falsified and there's no way he could have gotten access to them on his own.

"The Italians are concerned because the dig site that Sam was working on is of great historic significance. It's called the Emerald Bower of Claudius, and it's one of the most important archaeological finds of this century in Rome. Sam was working with a team of students from Rochester, and the Italians suspect that one or more of them may have been Sam's accomplices.

"They are particularly worried because, to date, no one has uncovered the one artifact that everyone was expecting to find right away: the Emerald-Eyed Lions of Emperor Claudius. The authorities are afraid they might have been stolen already."

A new picture came on the screen. It was an old-looking painting of two lion statues. At least, I assumed they were supposed to be lions. They looked sort of like a cross between a lion and a pug dog. They were made of some kind of yellow metal and had huge green eyes.

"It's not common knowledge, but there was a theft ring that operated at another Italian archaeological site six years ago, and managed to make off with several priceless antiquities. The Italians want to prevent this from happening again at all costs. Your mission is to infiltrate the dig, posing as archaeology students, and see what you can find out about a possible theft ring."

"Archaeology students?" I sputtered. The sum total of what I knew about archaeology was how to spell it, and even that I wasn't too sure about. How were we supposed to pass as any kind of experts?

"See too if you can locate the Emerald-Eyed Lions," the voiceover went on. "And above all, *be discreet*. ATAC is involved precisely because we want this taken care of quietly, under the official radar. The Italians have gotten very touchy about foreigners looting their art and artifacts, and we are trying to keep the situation from getting worse.

"You fly to Rome this evening. Your plane tickets and other travel documents will be delivered in a separate package. Once you arrive in Rome, you'll receive dig kits and a further briefing on the dig. We're counting on you, Frank and Joe. As usual, this disk will be reformatted in five seconds."

A graphic of a clock appeared on the screen, with the second hand counting down from five to zero. A moment later the screen went blank.

"We're going to Rome?" Joe said, his eyebrows rising. "Score! Road trip!"

"I guess we are," I said slowly. "I just wish we had more to go on. This ATAC briefing is even skimpier than usual."

"No sweat, we'll figure it out like we always do," Joe said confidently. "Don't look so serious, bro! Isn't this what you wanted? I doubt we're going to run into any masked wrestlers or biker thugs on an archaeological dig!"

As I thought that one over, I started to grin. "You have a point," I said. "An excellent point."

Excitement was bubbling up in my gut. We were on a mission, and we were headed to Italy, too!

My grin widened. I loved this job!

CHAPTER 2

NANCY

ROMAN HOLIDAY

"This morning I thought we'd visit the Palatine Hill. The Palatine is the place where the legendary fore-fathers of Rome—Romulus and Remus—supposedly were found by the she-wolf who nursed them. It was also the site of most of the homes and palaces of the early Roman emperors."

"It sounds amazing, Aunt Estelle," I said.

"Nancy Drew, I am surprised to hear such lazy adjectival usage from you," Aunt Estelle told me a bit severely. "The word 'amazing' should not be used as a substitute for 'interesting' or 'fascinating.' Its meaning has more to do with being startled or shocked. I know that many young people today are, shall we say, cavalier in their use of overheated vocabulary to convey perfectly ordinary sentiments, but I believe *you* can do better."

I could feel my cheeks reddening. "Um—sorry, I think." I glanced at my friends Bess and George for help.

"Don't look at us," George told me. "Just accept it."

"I would if I understood what it meant," I retorted.

Aunt Estelle unexpectedly burst out laughing. "Touché!" she exclaimed. "I'm sorry, dear. I was being pompous."

"Aunt" Estelle isn't actually my aunt. She's the great aunt of George Fayne and Bess Marvin, who are my best friends and also happen to be each other's cousins. I call her Aunt Estelle because she asked me to. "It's just what I'm used to," she said.

For a great aunt, she's very cool. In her late sixties, she lives in New York City by herself (she never married) and spends a lot of her time traveling. Not long ago, she announced that she wanted to take Bess and George to Rome with her. She invited me to come along too. "All young people should spend time in Europe," she'd said firmly. "It's imperative for their education."

Although she has kind of an old-fashioned manner sometimes, Aunt Estelle can also be wickedly funny. And though I didn't know her that well, she'd always been super nice to me. I was really glad I'd had the free time to come on this trip. It doesn't happen that often.

I'm an amateur detective, see. Even though I'm still

a teenager, I'm well known enough that people in my home town, River Heights, seek me out when they have a mystery the police can't handle for whatever reason. It seems like I almost always have a case to solve. But for once my slate was empty, so I'd booked my flight to Italy with a clear conscience.

We'd been here three days already, and we'd been doing some serious sightseeing. Yesterday we'd spent all day at the Vatican museum, viewing its incredible collection of medieval and Renaissance art, and the day before we'd gone to the Palazzo Barberini—another art museum—and the Villa Borghese gardens. Aunt Estelle knew everything there was to know about the history and culture of Rome.

We were staying in the elegant pensione, or apartment, of one of Aunt Estelle's old friends, Ugo Artom. Bess, George, and I trooped down the spiral staircase to the courtyard while Aunt Estelle took the elevator. In most Roman buildings, the elevator is only big enough for one or two people—I guess because the buildings were built way before electric power became common, and so when the elevators were added they had to squeeze them into whatever space was free.

We stepped out into brilliant sunshine. Though it was only May, it already felt like summer. I paused to put on the sunglasses I'd bought the day before. They were some Italian brand that Bess told me was very chic. I checked my reflection in a shop window. Not bad! My reddish blond hair was pulled back into a loose braid, and I wore black low-waist pants with leather sandals and a black sleeveless top. The combination of the outfit and the oversize glasses made me look mysterious, like a movie star in disguise.

We set off. Our apartment was in a building right by the Tiber river, on the side called Trastevere. "Look at that!" George exclaimed as we walked past a section of ancient-looking brick wall. "I can't get over how you can just walk right past all this stuff that's hundreds of years old!"

"I know," I agreed. "There's just so much history here—layers and layers of it. It's everywhere!"

Aunt Estelle led us across a small footbridge and then eastward into the maze of narrow streets with buildings painted in pale earth tones that make up the center of Rome. None of the streets seems to go in anything like a straight line. It's amazing to me that Aunt Estelle never seems to get lost.

"There's the Temple of Hercules Victor," she told us as we passed a small, round building with weathered marble pillars. A wrought-iron fence protected it from visitors. "It's the oldest marble building we know of in Rome. It dates from about 120 B.C."

I quickly did the math. Wow. That little building was over two thousand years old!

"It's just standing there by the street," Bess marveled.

"And that temple down there, past the fountain, is the called the Temple of Portunus, the god of the port." Aunt Estelle shook her head. "You know, when I was the age you girls are now, there weren't even fences around these sites, let alone guards or admission fees. Why, I remember wandering through the Forum and sitting down to eat my lunch on a bit of marble that turned out to be the head of the emperor Trajan!"

"I hope you didn't drop any tuna salad on him," George said with a grin.

Aunt Estelle chuckled. "If I did, I hope he took it as an offering."

We walked on, with Aunt Estelle pointing out the historical sights, from ancient temples to medieval churches to Renaissance fountains.

"And we haven't even gotten to the big historical site yet," Bess whispered to me. "When are we going to get to go shoe shopping?"

I grinned. "When they start building shoe stores inside the ruins," I whispered back.

I'd been reading a bit about the major sites of ancient Rome in my guidebook. "Weren't some new things recently discovered on the Palatine Hill?" I asked as we headed along a wide avenue.

"They were indeed. A few years ago, there was the Domus Aurea—Nero's Golden House, as we call it in

English," Aunt Estelle explained. "Also, in early 2007, a grotto believed to be the lost shrine of Romulus and Remus was uncovered. And then, only a few months ago, there was a third very exciting find—the so-called Emerald Bower of the Emperor Claudius. That site is not yet open to the public, as the archaeologists are still excavating it. But we'll be able to see a bit of their work, I think."

We were picking our way now through the outskirts of the Forum, the market area of ancient Rome. Masses of tourists milled around us, looking sunburned and happy. Cameras clicked and I heard snatches of at least six different languages. Hawkers selling souvenirs called out their wares. Near the Colosseum, a man dressed in the leather armor and plumed helmet of an ancient Roman soldier posed for photos with passersby.

A woman wearing a colorful embroidered blouse and a headscarf stepped in front of me. *"Il povero bambino,"* she said to me, and held out a crying baby. *"Per favore, signorina!"*

I stepped back, startled, and Aunt Estelle took my arm with a firm grip. *"Basta,"* she said to the woman, and pulled me away. "I should warn you, my dears, that the pickpockets of Rome are legendary," she told us. "That woman was almost certainly one of them. A favorite trick is to hand you a crying baby and then, while you are holding it and therefore off guard, to deftly rob you of your wallet."

"Whoa," George said with a whistle. "That's creepy!"

We paid the entrance fee and began climbing the steps set into the slope of the Palatine Hill. It was less crowded here, and as we moved up the hill, Bess gave a little cry of delight. "Look!" she said, pointing. I followed the direction of her finger and saw, set into the hillside, a little cave with a tinkling natural spring inside. Cool, moist air wafted out and stirred Bess's blond hair around her face. "The air smells like a forest," she said.

"Mmm, it is nice," I agreed.

"Isn't it lovely?" Aunt Estelle said. "And just ahead is the palace of Augustus, the first of the Roman emperors." She pointed farther up the hill.

It *was* amazing, I thought. You couldn't walk two feet in Rome without tripping over a huge piece of history!

"First of the Roman emperors?" George repeated. "Why wasn't Romulus or Remus the first emperor, since they founded the city? Why this Augustus guy?"

"Rome began as a republic, actually," Aunt Estelle explained. "It had a senate, two elected leaders called consuls, and various other bodies that were supposed to govern it, and it worked that way for several hundred years. But by the time of Julius Caesar, the republic had grown very large and spread out, and thus much harder to govern. It nearly collapsed in civil war as various powerful men—Caesar was only one of them—tried to gain control of the city and the Roman army. There was a period of instability for several years, and it only ended when Caesar's adopted son Octavian took over, changed his name to Augustus, and proclaimed himself emperor."

"Wow." George was silent as she digested the history lesson.

We continued up to the top of the hill, which was a flat area the size of several football fields. Though we were in the middle of the city, up here there were no cars or buses, and you could hear grasshoppers droning in the long grass. All around us lay huge slabs and pillars of marble, remnants of the palaces where Rome's rulers had lived so long ago. You could see the outlines of massive, stately buildings in the ground. Pine and cypress trees scented the warm air. It was peaceful and a little bit sad.

"I can almost imagine that we're back in ancient Rome right now," Bess said in a hushed voice.

"I know what you mean," I agreed. "It's easy to picture the buildings that used to be here. They must have been huge!"

"The ancient Romans didn't think small," George commented.

"The new excavation, Claudius's Emerald Bower, is

this way," Aunt Estelle said, leading us forward and to the left. "It's in the fold between the Palatine and the Caelian Hills. Shall we have a quick look?"

As we followed her, she continued her lecture on Roman history.

"Now, Claudius was the grandson of Augustus, and he came to the throne after the death of the mad emperor Caligula," she told us. "For many years Claudius was believed to have been a bit slow witted, but modern historians have revised their opinion of him quite a bit. He was a reasonably effective emperor, neither the best nor the worst of his clan, less of a spendthrift than Caligula but not the natural leader of men that Augustus or, for that matter, Tiberius had been."

"How do you *remember* all this stuff, Aunt Estelle?" Bess burst out. "You're making my brain hurt!"

Aunt Estelle raised her eyebrows. "Am I boring you?"

"That's not what I meant," Bess protested.

"No way," George said. "We're not bored."

"Oh, no!" I hastened to add. "Just a little over-whelmed."

"I'm pleased to say that you're all dreadful liars," Aunt Estelle told us with a smile. "But thank you for humoring an old lady."

"The history is interesting, Aunt Estelle," Bess said.

"It really is. But I also think modern Rome is exciting. And I'd like to see some of it—just for a change of pace."

"I understand," Aunt Estelle said. "Modern Rome is wonderful, it's true. And I absolutely agree that you girls should explore it. So I think this afternoon I'll visit with my old friend Vittorio diLanza while you three go off on your own. How does that sound?"

"Great!" we all said together.

"Another 'old friend,' Aunt Estelle?" George added with a wicked grin. "Like Ugo Artom? How many gentleman friends do you have in this town, and are you sure you don't need a chaperone?"

"Oh, don't be silly," Aunt Estelle chided, but I noticed her cheeks turned slightly pink. I grinned to myself. Touché, George!

The hill began to slope down. Ahead of us I could now see what looked like a construction site. A couple of trailers sat on a clear stretch of ground next to a large roped-off area of freshly dug earth. Lengths of string divided it into several smaller quadrants. In each quadrant, three or four people squatted with tiny picks or brushes in their hands, painstakingly sifting through the soil. At one end of the site, I could make out the remains of some brick walls and what looked like a doorway.

"I don't think we can go any closer than this," Aunt

Estelle said as we halted several yards away. "As I mentioned, the dig site is not open to the public yet."

"So this was the Emperor Claudius's weekend house," I said. After the grand scale of the buildings on top of the hill, this one looked decidedly modest.

"Hey, Nan," Bess said in a low voice. "Check out that blond guy in the square to my left. He's cute."

I looked. I couldn't see the guy's face, but he had tousled, slightly shaggy blond hair and tanned, muscular arms set off by his white T-shirt. He wore a red bandana as a sweatband around his head. Definitely Bess's type.

"You know who he reminds me of?" Bess mused. "Joe Hardy. Remember Joe and his brother Frank?"

"Of course I do," I said. How could I forget? Joe and Frank Hardy were teen detectives like me. They worked for a secret organization called ATAC—American Teens Against Crime. We'd met them at a rock concert a while ago where they were working undercover on a case. I'd gotten involved too, and we'd ended up making friends. They were great guys, both of them.

I squinted at the blond guy. He really did remind me of Joe Hardy—same build, same haircut, same style.

My gaze moved over the other quadrants—and stopped on one to my right, where a taller, slightly wirier guy with short dark hair was working. He wore a checked button-down shirt, open at the neck. Hah!

He reminded me of Frank! Frank was the older and more . . . well, buttoned-down of the brothers. Imagine, someone that looked like Joe and someone that looked like Frank in the same place. Funny coincidence.

Or was it? As I stared at him, the dark-haired guy straightened up and turned in our direction, wiping sweat from his forehead.

My mouth fell open as I took in his thin face and dark eyes.

"I don't believe it," I said. "It *is* him! That's Frank Hardy!"

CHAPTER 3

JOE

DIGGING FOR CLUES

The sun burned down on the back of my neck. "Man, it's hot," I muttered, setting down my pick and taking another sip from my water bottle.

"But isn't it so fantastic to be here?" Kyra, one of my dig-mates gushed.

"Oh, yeah, it's fantastic all right," I agreed quickly, doing my best to summon up a sincere smile. It helped that Kyra was about twenty and cute, with glowing cocoa-colored skin, wild black curls, and golden brown eyes.

"So, Joe, I never saw you around the archaeology department back at school," she commented. "Where were you hiding yourself?"

"Actually, Frank and I don't go to Rochester. We're

students at Sanderton, in Arizona," I lied. This was the cover story ATAC had given Frank and me. "One of our professors used to teach at Rochester, though, and he was able to get us onto this dig at the last moment."

"Wow, you're so lucky," Kyra said. "It's really hard to get onto the digs at Rochester. I applied for three years in a row before I got on this one. It must be like a dream come true for you!"

"Did you say you're from Sanderton?" called one of the other archaeology students, a pudgy, red-faced guy named Arthur. He walked over and stood beaming at me. "I used to go there!"

Uh-oh! This could be awkward. . . . Still, I was confident I could avoid any serious mistakes. I'm good at thinking on my feet.

"I transferred to Rochester to be with my girlfriend," Arthur went on. His smile faded. "Then she dumped me."

I hid a grin. "That's a serious bummer, dude."

"Yeah, well, her loss," he muttered. His eyes brightened. "Hey, what did you think of Professor Tayler's course?"

"Tayler?" I figured the best way out of this was to lie as little as possible. "Um, I haven't taken his class yet."

"Haven't taken it?" Arthur's forehead furrowed. "But it's the intro to archaeology—you have to take it before you can declare your major."

Whoops. I was trying to think of a reasonable reply when I heard a girl's voice shouting behind me. "Frank!" she cried. "Frank and Joe, is that really you?"

I spun around. What now?

Standing on the hill a few yards up from us was a group of three girls. Three hot girls. There was a redhead in fashionable black clothes and movie-star shades and a slim, athletic-looking brunette. The one who was waving at me and my brother was blond and curvy, with big blue eyes and dimples.

I recognized those dimples. . . .

"Bess Marvin!" I called, breaking into a grin. I hopped over the string that marked my quadrant and jogged up the slope toward Bess and her friends. "And Nancy Drew, and George Fayne!" I stopped in front of them, noticing for the first time the gray-haired lady with them. "And, uh—"

"Estelle Baxter-Collins," the old lady said, giving me the once-over from sharp green eyes. "I'm George and Bess's great aunt."

"Pleased to meet you." I gave her my most charming smile. Old ladies love me. Although this one was looking a tad skeptical.

Frank came up next to me, his expression both pleased and worried. I could guess what was going through my big bro's mind. He was thrilled to see the girls again—especially Nancy. Though he wouldn't admit it, I was fairly sure he had a little crush on her. Frank goes gaga for smart girls. And Nancy was super cute on top of that. But he was also worried that one of the girls would say something to blow our cover here. And he was worried that he wouldn't know what to say to them. And he was worried that the dig supervisor would get mad at us for leaving our quadrants. And he was probably also worried about something totally irrelevant, like global warming.

Frank worries a lot.

Bess was introducing us to her aunt. "This is Joe, and this is Frank," she said. "The H—"

"Hamilton brothers," Frank cut in smoothly. Bess's eyes widened and then I saw realization on her face. Frank held out his hand to Aunt Estelle. "It's nice to meet you."

"Likewise," Aunt Estelle said.

George gave me a light punch in the arm. "I can't believe we ran into you. What are you doing in Rome, of all places?"

I was about to answer "working on the dig," but Frank beat me to it.

"Working on the dig," he said quickly, and gave me a hard stare.

I glared back. "That's what I was about to say," I muttered. "For college," I added pointedly, sticking to our cover story even though it was stupid. Nancy and her friends knew we weren't in college. The only person we were fooling was Aunt Estelle, and I couldn't see how it could possibly matter if she knew the truth.

"For college, huh?" Nancy's blue eyes had a glint in them that I'd seen before. It was obvious to her that we were here working on a mission, and she wanted to know all about it. "I'd love to hear more. Hey, can you guys take a break? We'll buy you a cappuccino while you tell us all about the . . . dig."

I for one had no problem with filling Nancy in on the case. She's a great detective, and she might have some good ideas for us. Plus, I'd much rather sit in a café and talk to three cute girls than dig in the dirt under the hot Roman sun for another hour. "That sounds great," I said quickly, before Frank could object. "We're due for a break anyway."

"I don't know . . . ," Frank began, but I cut him off.

"It'll be fine," I said. "I'll tell Vanessa." Vanessa was our dig supervisor.

Aunt Estelle cleared her throat. "Well," she said, "I'm a bit fatigued. I think I'll go back to the pensione for a bit of a rest while you young people catch up. Girls, don't forget, we're meeting Ugo for dinner at eight, so please be back at the pensione by seven. Frank, Joe, it was lovely to meet you and I hope to see you again soon."

"You too," we both said.

I hurried back to the dig and found Vanessa, our supervisor, muttering into her cell phone. She snapped it shut as I walked up and turned to me, adjusting her rectangular-framed glasses.

Vanessa was an Englishwoman in her thirties who, in the few hours that we'd been here, had already struck me as someone who wasn't very good at enjoying life. She looked constantly harassed and irritable, and she'd already yelled at me for not being careful enough with my little pick. She seemed to spend most of her time on the phone, rather than working on the dig.

"If you want to take a break I can't stop you," she snapped when I told her what Frank and I were doing. "You're volunteers, after all. But try not to be too long, right?"

"We'll be back before you know it," I promised.

"Hmmm." Vanessa sniffed.

I hurried back to the girls and we all headed down the hill to a café Frank and I had eaten at that morning.

"Okay," Nancy said when we'd been seated at a shady table and had all ordered our drinks. She leaned forward and put her chin on her clasped hands. "So tell us, are you here on an ATAC mission?"

Frank looked uneasy. "Well . . . ," he began.

I shook my head. "Frank, chill. We can tell Nancy, Bess, and George what we're doing. They're practically ATAC agents themselves."

"We're not going to blow your cover," Nancy assured him, her blue eyes twinkling.

Frank's neck flushed and he gave a sheepish grin. "No, I know you aren't," he admitted, leaning back in his seat. "I guess Joe is right."

"A first!" I declared. "Frank Hardy admits Joe is correct!"

Bess giggled. But Frank shushed me. "Don't say that name too loud," he cautioned. "We're the Hamiltons here, remember?"

"Whatever." I personally couldn't see what difference it made if we used our real names on this mission. Who in Rome was going to recognize us? But ATAC insisted on aliases, and Frank was a stickler for the rules.

The waiter set down our coffees. "Here's the deal," I explained when he'd walked away. "We're trying to figure out whether there's a theft ring at the dig, stealing artifacts."

Frank chimed in and we told the girls about Sam Lewis, the things he'd tried to sell online, and the Italian authorities' fear that he wasn't working alone. "He seems really scared about something," Frank added. "He's refusing to cooperate with the Italian police, even though it could only help him."

"What do you know about him?" Nancy asked.

"Nothing out of the ordinary," I told her. "He's a

college junior and an archaeology major. He came here for the dig. One possible lead is that he was traveling with his girlfriend, Caitlin Boggs, also a Rochester student, but the authorities have lost track of her since she came to Rome. She was supposedly staying in a pensione on the Quirinal Hill, but she skipped out without paying her bill after the first night and no one knows where she went."

"So you'll definitely want to find her and ask her some questions," Nancy commented, raising her eyebrows.

"She's tops on our list," Frank confirmed. "The other strange thing is that Sam disappeared from the dig a couple of days before he was arrested. Everyone just assumed he and Caitlin took off somewhere together. But then he turned up again when he got arrested. He won't say what he was doing in the mean time.

"We're trying to find out more about Sam and Caitlin from the other students on the dig. But Caitlin wasn't an archaeology student, wasn't working on the dig, and so far no one seems to know much about her."

"We just started this morning, though," I pointed out.

"Speaking of working on the dig, how did you guys get in on it?" George wanted to know.

"And can we do it too?" Nancy added eagerly.

"Sorry." Frank shook his head. "ATAC had to pull

lots of strings to get us our spots. It's apparently got a long waiting list. And we had to take a crash course in archaeology. We're still faking it, but if no one asks us tough questions, we can get by."

"Check out our gear," I said, reaching for my backpack. "Some of it's pretty awesome!" I pulled out a small hammer and a set of brushes. "Not this stuff. But how about this?" I held up a Geiger counter and waved it over Bess. It didn't click. "Nope, you're not radioactive," I told her.

She flashed her dimples at me. "That's a relief! What do you need that thing for, anyway? Are you trying to detect ancient Roman bombs?"

"No," Frank said, laughing. "The Geiger counters are for use in radiocarbon dating. That's a method we use to figure out the age of artifacts. See, radioactive carbon occurs in nature, and its half-life—"

"Don't get technical, Frank," I interrupted. "All we need to know is, it beeps when it finds radioactivity." I took out a pad of paper. "And then there's this."

"Paper?" George said, arching her eyebrows. "Radical new invention."

"Ah, but it's not just any paper." I grabbed a pen and jotted down GEORGE FAYNE LOVES JOE HARDY.

"You wish!" George laughed.

"Watch this." I folded the sheet of paper and stuck it into my water glass.

"Oh, is that how you treat my friend's feelings?" Bess teased.

I grinned. "Just wait." I gave it ten or fifteen seconds, then fished out the wet page. Unfolding it, I showed the girls that the writing was still as crisp as ever. It hadn't even smeared. And the paper hadn't turned to pulp, either.

"Completely waterproof," Frank said happily.

"Cool!" George, Nancy, and Bess all said together.

I waggled my eyebrows at George. "Guess this means you're going to love me forever," I teased her.

"Like I said before, you wish." George punched me lightly in the arm, her cheeks pink.

Frank was checking his watch. "Sorry, but I think Joe and I had better get back to work," he said.

"Let's meet up later," Nancy suggested. "We have a dinner tonight, as you heard, but maybe we could get together tomorrow for lunch."

"Sounds great," Frank agreed, and I nodded.

We settled on a restaurant that Bess had read about, I Tre Merli, not too far away from the dig. Then we headed back up the hill and got back to work on our quadrants. The day had grown even hotter—after fifteen minutes my shirt was soaked with sweat. I was working alongside Kyra. Arthur, luckily, was nowhere in sight, so I didn't have to worry about more awkward questions about my "college" experience.

"So how long have you been working on this dig?" I asked as I chipped at a clod of hardened mud with my little pick. *Thunk. Thunk.* "Found anything good yet?"

"Five weeks," Kyra told me. "I haven't found anything yet, but we've barely scratched the surface. It'll probably be the better part of a year before we excavate the whole structure."

A year! I tried to imagine squatting in the dirt, sifting through dirt, breathing in dirt, staring at more dirt like this every day for the next several months. *Thunk. Thunk.*

I decided I'd rather be boiled alive.

"This quadrant could have some really important finds in it," Kyra went on. "I'm sure you've studied all the layouts, so you know that we're almost definitely excavating Claudius's tablinum."

Tablinum . . . tablinum . . . I searched frantically through the jumble of facts we'd been force-fed by ATAC just two days ago. Was the tablinum a room? A piece of furniture? No good. I was drawing a complete blank. "Yeah, that's really cool," was my brilliant comeback.

I decided to probe a little. "So has anyone found anything really valuable thing yet?" I asked. "You know, gold, jewels, that kind of thing?"

Kyra shrugged. "Not that I know of. You make it sound like we're on a treasure hunt. We're not—we're looking for history."

"But some treasure would be pretty cool, you have to admit," I said with a grin. "Or are you saying that if I find a gold necklace lying around, no one will miss it if I just stick it in my pocket?"

Kyra frowned. "I don't think that's very funny," she said.

"Come on, I can't believe no one ever tries it," I said. "Little things must go missing from archaeological digs all the time. You know, old coins and medallions and stuff." Like the stuff Sam Lewis had tried to sell.

"I wouldn't know," Kyra said coldly, and turned her back on me.

Plink! My pick rang on some kind of rock. Remembering what I'd been told, I put the pick down and took up my trowel instead. I scraped gently at layers of soil, clearing it away from a grayish bit of smooth stone. "Hey," I said, feeling an unexpected spurt of enthusiasm, "I think I found something."

Kyra, forgetting she was offended, turned around. "What?" she demanded, craning over my shoulder.

I picked up the whisk-broom and swept more dry earth aside. Reaching down, I gently extracted the chunk of stone from the ground. "It looks like a head," I said, studying it. It was deeply weathered, with features so worn away they were hard to recognize as someone's face.

"Wow." Kyra's voice was full of wonder.

"Put that down!" an English-accented voice said sharply. I glanced up. Vanessa was glaring down at me.

"Don't you know not to take an artifact out of the ground until it's been photographed?" she said.

Whoops! I *had* been told that. "Sorry, I guess I just got carried away," I said.

"Mmph." Vanessa didn't look any happier. She fitted the stone head back into the ground, pulled out a Polaroid camera, and took shots from various angles.

"It's an ancestral bust," Kyra volunteered. "The shape is exactly like a head of Emperor Augustus that I saw in the Vatican Museum."

"It's nothing of the sort," Vanessa snapped. "The crudeness of the sculpting suggests it's from a later era, perhaps ninth or tenth century A.D. It's medieval, not Imperial."

"But the laurel wreath on the—," Kyra objected.

Vanessa cut her off. "It's imitation. Really, I think I know more about the subject than you." Unearthing the head again, she carried it off toward one of the trailers.

"Miss Congeniality," I said under my breath as I watched her go.

"She can be pretty nasty, it's true," Kyra agreed ruefully. "The thing is, she really is an expert on artifacts from the Imperial era. But she's wrong about this one. That's an Imperial-era bust of Augustus, I'm sure of it."

"Well, people make mistakes," I pointed out.

Kyra shook her head. "That's a big mistake for someone like Vanessa. With her experience and knowledge, I'm surprised."

Hmmm. I stared after Vanessa with sudden interest. Mistake—or misdirection? Could she be deliberately trying to make us believe we'd found something worthless?

As I watched her, I saw Vanessa stop, take out her cell phone, and press it to her ear once again. I decided maybe it was worth trying to hear what she was saying.

"Be right back," I told Kyra, and I hopped over the string that marked the edge of our quadrant. Vanessa was standing near a row of portable toilets, so I pretended I was going to use one. Stepping inside, I held my breath against the stink and climbed up so that my ear was against the vent.

"Look, I told you, I don't have the money yet," I heard Vanessa saying. "I'm doing everything I— No, I *will* have it for you, I just need another couple of days!" Her voice had a ragged edge to it.

Interesting. Very interesting. So Vanessa desperately needed money.

And Vanessa was either making mistakes or lying about valuable artifacts.

Put them together and what did you get?

Maybe, just maybe, you got a thief.

CHAPTER 4

FRANK

SUAVE WITH THE LADIES

When I got back to the dig, I found that a new volunteer had arrived while I was gone. He was a tall, slightly stooped man who looked about fifty years old. He wore khaki shorts and a pith helmet, so he looked kind of like one of those safari hunters in an old movie. His craggy face was dominated by deep-set dark eyes.

As I walked up he was standing with his trowel dangling from his hand, talking to one of the other volunteers, a girl called Margaret. "Well, of course, Claudius was one of the great scholars of his time," he was saying. "He certainly read several languages, and I believe he kept up correspondence with at least six or seven prominent philosophers across the empire. As a young man, he studied with the historian Pliny."

"Uh-huh," Margaret said. She had a slightly glazed expression on her face.

"Who's the new guy?" I asked Jeff, the fourth volunteer on our quadrant, in a low voice. "No way he's a college student."

"His name's Claude Bonaire," Jeff whispered back. "No, he's not a student. He's strictly an amateur. Here because he's obsessed with the emperor Claudius." He rolled his eyes. "And I do mean obsessed. He'll talk your ear off if you let him."

"How'd he get a spot on the dig if he's not a student?" I wanted to know.

Jeff held up his hand and rubbed the fingers together. "Money talks," he said. "Bonaire is some kind of multimillionaire in the shipping industry. From what I heard, he's practically financing this dig single-handed, so if he wants to come out and play archaeologist, of course no one's going to tell him he can't."

"I guess not," I replied.

"Not that he does a lot of actual work," Jeff added. "Mostly he just stands around and talks. There was this guy working on the dig before. Dude named Sam. For some reason Bonaire really liked to lecture him." He laughed. "It got so every time Sam saw Bonaire coming, he'd try to hide."

"Sam?" I said casually, though my interest had

perked up. "You mean the guy I replaced? I heard he got arrested. What's the deal with that?"

Jeff shrugged. "I was pretty surprised when I heard about him stealing artifacts. He always seemed serious about archaeology to me. But I didn't really know him well. You know, most of us hang out with each other when we're not working, but Sam never did, because he was always with that girlfriend of his—Caitlin. They were practically joined at the hip. And she didn't seem very interested in archaeology, even though she was always hanging around here at first, distracting Sam."

"At first?" I raised my eyebrows. "Why'd she stop?"

"Who knows?" Jeff said. "I think Sam said she got a job. I did get the impression they were kind of short of cash. But then, we all are." He grinned. "That's what being a student is all about, right?" His grin faded. "I guess that's what made Sam do what he did."

"Maybe so. So was this Caitlin staying at the university?" I asked. All the volunteers on the dig crew had been given places in the dorms in a local university. Joe and I were sharing a room.

"No, Sam was, but Caitlin wasn't allowed to since she wasn't with the crew," Jeff said. "I don't know where she was staying." He shook his head. "There was something kind of shifty about that girl. She was pretty enough, and nice enough, but I just got a weird vibe off her."

Interesting. I filed that away.

Margaret and Bonaire joined us, and the conversation shifted to other things—mainly the emperor Claudius. It was true, Bonaire did seem kind of obsessed with the guy, but I also found what he had to say interesting. He really knew his stuff. "Claudius was completely misunderstood throughout history," he told me. "Because he limped and had a speech impediment, people believed he was an idiot. But he was really a very capable administrator. Unfortunately, with a couple of exceptions, most of the scholarship about the period still tends to overlook him."

We worked for a couple of hours, sifting through the dry, heat-baked soil, looking for shards of pottery or bits of carved stone or metal. There was something very satisfying about being out here under the sun, searching for clues from the distant past. I liked it.

But I wasn't really here to be an archaeologist, much as I was enjoying it. Joe and I had a mission. Which meant I should get cracking.

I glanced around my quadrant. I'd probably gotten all the information I could about Sam out of Jeff. Margaret might have something to add, but I didn't want to make Jeff suspicious by harping too much on Sam and Caitlin. And Bonaire, though he'd apparently spent some time talking to Sam, seemed an unlikely candidate for involvement in a theft ring.

After all, he was already insanely rich. Why would he need to steal artifacts?

To tell the truth, I didn't think any of them were likely candidates for this crime. Maybe I should be working at it from another angle. We knew from our ATAC briefing that the pieces Sam tried to sell had already been logged at the dig site and, presumably, taken to the warehouse where all the artifacts were being stored. The warehouse was owned by a shipping company called BS&T, which was in charge of shipping selected artifacts to England for a display in a London Museum.

It seemed reasonable to assume that maybe Sam had an accomplice at the shipping company. Joe and I had planned to investigate the place, and as I thought about it, I decided now was the time.

I glanced around for Joe to let him know what I was planning, but I didn't see him or Vanessa, the dig supervisor, anywhere. "Do me a favor," I said to Jeff. "I've got an errand to run that will probably take me the rest of the afternoon. Would you let Vanessa know I had to take off a little early?"

"No problem," Jeff said. "See you later."

I shouldered my backpack and headed toward the nearest Metro stop, pulling out my cell phone as I went. ATAC had given us cool satellite phones that worked not just in the United States, but anywhere in the world that had cell service. Plus they had all kinds of sweet extras, like a built-in homing device, a high-quality camera, and a function that let you broadcast any sounds in your immediate area to a listener on the other end. Oh, and of course, they had Internet access.

I sent Joe a text message: going to check out bs&t offices, meet you at dorm later. Then I hopped on the Metro.

I took the Metro to the local train station and caught a train for Civitavecchia, which was the port city where BS&T had its offices. The ride was almost an hour long, which meant I'd be arriving there pretty close to closing time, but it couldn't be helped.

I spent the ride staring out the window at the Italian countryside. The area around Rome is kind of built up, but it still seemed pretty exotic to me. The land was mostly flat, divided into plots by hedges made of narrow, pointy evergreen trees. The farther from the city we got, the more the suburban sprawl gave way to farms. Most of the houses were low to the ground, with red tile roofs and warm blue or gold stucco walls. Here and there, herds of cows grazed. And once, in the distance, I spotted a row of immense stone arches striding across a field. I felt a twinge of excitement. That had to be part of the ancient Roman aqueduct network!

This is the kind of mission I could stand more of, I

thought. *Travel, see the world—and so far no one has tried to turn me into ground meat! I'm loving it!*

At last the train arrived at Civitavecchia. I made my way toward the docks, figuring that was where BS&T would have its office. Once I got there, I used my tiny stock of Italian phrases to ask directions and, amazingly, found the BS&T office right away.

The office was a prefab building that stood a little ways back from the dock, next to a warehouse with a tin roof and a long row of loading bays. One or two trucks were parked in the bays, but I couldn't see anyone in them or in the warehouse. The whole place looked pretty sleepy.

I had a basic cover story prepared, but after that I would just have to wing it. I had no idea who I'd meet here or what connection, if any, they'd have to our mission. But I hoped I'd be able to strike up a conversation with whoever I met and learn something that way. Squaring my shoulders, I walked into the office.

The place was functional but not luxurious, with upholstered visitor's chairs facing a couple of desks. The walls were covered with framed posters of ships throughout the ages, everything from Roman triremes up to modern tankers and cargo vessels. A flag I didn't recognize, white with a black silhouetted head wearing a white headband in the middle, hung near the back wall.

A young woman with long black hair tied back in a loose ponytail sat at one of the desks, frowning at a computer screen. The nameplate on the desk read JOANNA PAOLI. *"Buon giorno,"* I said to her. I searched for the right words in Italian. *"Me despiace, ma non parlo—"*

"I speak English," she interrupted, not returning the smile. She gave me a severe look, and I couldn't help noticing that her eyes were green, with long black lashes. She was very pretty.

"Oh. Well, good," I said, a little flustered. Pretty girls do that to me. "Uh—I'm from the dig on the Palatine Hill. Um, someone sent me down here to pick up a package."

"A package?" Joanna repeated. "That doesn't make sense. There is no package here. Who would send you to pick up a package from us?" Her accent was very good, and she spoke rapidly, the words coming out like bullets.

"Um—Vanessa?" I said, praying she wouldn't call Vanessa to check. "She, uh, she told someone else and someone else told me. Maybe I got the message wrong."

"You did," Joanna stated. "There is no package for Vanessa or anyone else here. You bring packages to us. We don't send packages to you." She turned back to her computer.

"Oh, well, uh, then I guess it's my mistake." I wasn't

doing so well in this conversation. "Um, what is it you do here? I mean, what's your connection to the dig?"

"We ship things," Joanna snapped. "For the dig and for our clients. We're a shipping company." She gave me another sharp look. "I'm closing the office now. You'll have to go."

"Right. Okay. Well, sorry I bothered you," I said. Hitching my backpack into a more comfortable position, I headed for the door. I could feel my neck turning red. *Very suave, Frank!* I'd struck out completely, and I hadn't learned a thing!

I could practically hear Joe's voice in my head, saying, "Leave schmoozing the pretty girls to me, big bro. You stick to the stuff you're good at." Or worse yet, Nancy Drew giving me that sympathetic smile of hers as she told me how she would have handled things.

Humiliating!

As I passed the warehouse I impulsively ducked into one of the loading bays. I had no idea what I was looking for, but I figured I might as well poke around inside, scope the place out, in the name of being thorough— otherwise this trip would have been a total waste.

The inside of the warehouse was shadowy, the air still and hot under the tin roof. Rough wooden palettes full of shipping crates were stacked one on top of the other in long rows, creating narrow alleys. Some of the palettes were covered in tarps, while others were bare.

The fluorescent lights that hung from the ceiling were all switched off.

"Hello?" I called. "Anyone here?"

No one answered. Good. I could snoop freely, then.

I prowled down one row and turned a corner, trying to read the labels on the shipping crates. But of course, in addition to being in Italian, they were obviously written in the usual industrial jargon, with lots of serial numbers and codes that meant nothing to me. I used my camera phone to snap a couple of pictures on the off chance that ATAC could learn something useful from them.

As I neared the back of the warehouse, I became aware of a sound coming from somewhere behind me. It sounded like a radio not tuned to any station—just pure static. But it was very faint, almost at the edge of hearing. I turned, trying to pinpoint where it was coming from.

Weird. It still seemed to be coming from behind me, even though I was facing the opposite direction now.

I turned again and crept forward a few steps. The sound seemed to move with me. What could it be?

Virtually no daylight from the open bays made its way back here, and all the overhead lamps were shut off, so it was pretty dark. I banged my shin on a shrouded crate and groaned softly in pain.

That's when a new sound joined the faint staticky

noise. A noise that was definitely coming from a point close to me, somewhere to my left. *Rrrrrrrrrrr. Rrrrrrrrrr.*

Growling. As in guard dog.

I winced. This could be a problem.

Then I heard yet another sound, this one to my right.

Rrrrrrrrr. Rrrrrrrrrrrrrr.

Make that plural—guard *dogs.*

And I was caught in between them.

CHAPTER 5

NANCY

TO CATCH A THIEF

"Oh, my gosh, everything is so incredibly beautiful here. I think I must be in heaven." Bess's voice was hushed.

I laughed. "That's the first time I've ever seen anyone have a religious experience in a leather goods store." Picking up a brown leather satchel, I stroked its buttery softness. Bess was right, the stuff in here was really special. Even though there were high-end leather stores in River Heights, somehow the merchandise looked more stylish here in Rome.

"I have a feeling this is the start of a whole afternoon of religious experiences," George drawled. "Bess has been talking about making a pilgrimage to the shops of Rome since we found out were going on this trip."

"I've been wanting to make a pilgrimage to the Italian fashion scene since I was six, thank you very much," Bess retorted. "Now if we can only persuade Aunt Estelle that we need to make a side visit to Milan . . ."

I put down the bag and walked over to a selection of men's wallets. *The slim black one would make a nice gift for my dad*, I thought. *Maybe I should get one for him—and one for my boyfriend, Ned, too.*

I reached to pick one up at the same time as another girl reached for it. Our hands bumped and I smiled an apology at her. She was shorter than me, with shoulder-length curly red hair and brown eyes in a heart-shaped face. She wore a green baby tee. Smiling back, she turned and drifted away.

I examined the wallets, and ended up choosing the black one for Ned and an oxblood one for my dad. Bess had picked out a small squared-off bag in bright aqua for herself, and even George had given in to the lure of the leather and bought herself a wide black belt with a heavy silver buckle.

"Clothes next," Bess said happily as we walked down crowded Via Condotti. Each shop we passed seemed to have the name of a famous designer on it. "And then shoes. Ooooh, the Enzo Garbone flagship store! We have to stop here, you guys! We can't afford anything in the store, but I just need to see the clothes up close. I've only ever seen them in magazines before."

We obediently followed Bess inside. Loud techno music pulsed from speakers overhead, and a shop assistant gave us a chilly smile from where she stood. The clothes on the racks seemed to be made exclusively of strips of torn fabric. I blinked as I caught sight of a headless mannequin decked out in a bomber jacket and a long burlap-strip skirt with high-heeled sandals. There was something just a little creepy about it.

"Interesting look," George murmured to me. "What did Bess say the designer's name was? Enzo Garbage?"

"George, be good," I whispered back, fighting the urge to giggle.

As Bess prowled reverently from rack to rack, I glanced out the window and caught sight of the girl from the leather store, the one who'd tried to pick up the same wallet I had. She was loitering on the sidewalk outside, checking out the window displays. I started to smile a greeting, but her eyes slid away from mine without any hint of recognition.

I shrugged. Guess she didn't remember me.

"Come on, Nancy, aren't you dying to try this on?" George asked. Turning, I saw that she was holding up a short skirt made of strips of suede alternating with strips of blue and green felt. The overall effect was sort of similar to one of those grass skirts you see in old Hawaiian beach movies.

I grinned. "I just don't think it's really me."

"Thank goodness for that," George shot back, and we both laughed.

After a few minutes we managed to pry Bess out of there, and we decided to search for an outdoor café to refresh ourselves with iced lattes. By this time we were at the Spanish Steps. Crowds of tourists thronged the famous staircase and the fountain in the shape of a sunken boat in the plaza. For a second I spotted a head of curly red hair and thought I was seeing the girl from the leather store yet again, but before I could make sure who it was, my view was blocked by a guy about my own age who stepped eagerly in front of me.

"*Cara mia*, you are so beautiful," he told me, grabbing my hand. "You will go out with me, yes? I take you to Italian disco." He mimed dancing.

"No, I won't," I said, trying not to smile as I pulled my hand free. "Sorry."

"But, baby!" he protested. "I think I love you!"

As I hurried away, flanked by Bess and George all three of us burst out laughing.

"Ah, now my Roman experience is complete," I joked.

Bess spotted a café and steered us toward it. We sat and ordered our drinks "Normally I would think any guy who behaved like that was a jerk," she said. "But that was just funny, not offensive. I wonder why?"

"When in Rome . . . ," George said with a shrug.

Our drinks arrived. "You know, I still can't believe we ran into Frank and Joe Hardy here," I mused. "Their case sounds interesting, don't you think?"

"I don't know about the case," George said. "But I can't believe that ATAC would actually send them to Rome! Talk about a sweet setup!"

"Do you think you'd like to work with ATAC, Nan?" Bess asked me.

I thought about that one. "Well, part of me is a little envious," I confessed. "I like all the support they get— you know, the case files, the gadgets, that stuff. But when I work on a mystery, part of what I love is knowing I'm helping someone. Seeing the relief on the face of the client when you tell them you solved their case is so great. Working for a big organization like that, I wonder if you start to feel removed from the actual people that you're trying to help. You know what I mean?" I swirled my straw around in the dregs of my latte. "Plus, I'm really enjoying being somewhere on an actual vacation for once, without a mystery."

"Amen!" Bess agreed. "The only mystery *I* want to solve is how I'm going to find myself a pair of Zucchero and Zenzero boots that don't cost a million dollars." She grinned. "But I *will* solve it before we leave Rome, mark my words!"

We sat for a bit longer, soaking up the sun and the atmosphere. Then George checked her watch. "It's five thirty," she told us. "We should probably head back to the pensione to meet Aunt Estelle soon. But we're right near the Trevi Fountain here, and I'm dying to see it. Want to walk over? I've heard it's just amazing."

"'Amazing' is a terribly sloppy adjective unless you mean shocking or surprising," I scolded, shaking my finger and trying to sound like Aunt Estelle.

George chuckled. "She is a trip, isn't she?"

We left some euros on the table to cover our bill and headed over the Via del Corso to the Fontana di Trevi. As we neared the fountain, the crowds grew thicker and thicker, to the point that we had a hard time staying together. Hawkers pushed through the throngs holding up postcards and other souvenirs.

"Watch your wallets, everyone," Bess warned, clutching the strap of her shoulder bag. "I heard this is one of the worst areas for pickpockets."

My own wallet was back in the pensione. I'd brought only some euro bills and a credit card, which I carried in a flat pouch that I wore around my neck under my shirt. I gripped my shopping bag more firmly.

"Check that out!" George exclaimed as the fountain came in sight. "Have you ever seen anything like it?"

The fountain seemed to be a natural outgrowth from the building that stood behind it. The central figure, a huge bearded god in a loincloth, stood in a niche in the wall of the building. Other gods and goddesses lounged around him on a craggy heap of stones and fallen pillars, all sculpted out of marble. A waterfall thundered over the stones and crashed into the blue pool, easily the size of a swimming pool, that lay beneath.

"It *is* amazing," I murmured, awestruck. "And I mean exactly that!"

Cameras clicked all around us. Apparently the other tourists felt the same way.

Suddenly I heard Bess give a cry of alarm. "My wallet!" she gasped. "It's gone!" I just felt someone bump into me and now my wallet is gone!"

"What?" Heart pounding, I spun around and scanned the crowd. I was looking for anyone who was moving away rapidly from where we were.

My eyes widened as, maybe five yards away, I caught sight of a mop of curly red hair and a green T-shirt. The girl from the leather store—again!

Coincidence?

I didn't think so. She'd been staking us out!

"George! Bess!" I said. "The girl with the red hair in the green shirt. We've got to head her off. You two go left, I'll go right. Don't let her out of your sight."

"Got it," George said, nodding. She grabbed Bess's hand and pushed through the crowd off to the left. I moved off at an angle, slipping between milling hordes.

"Excuse me," I murmured as I went. *"Me despiace. Perdóname. Excusez moi. Entschuldigung."* I used every language in which I knew how to say "excuse me," figuring that there probably were people here from most of the countries of Europe. Other countries, too, but I didn't know that many languages. . . .

All the while I strove to keep that redhead in my line of vision. Once the girl turned and checked over her shoulder. I glanced away so she wouldn't realize I'd seen her, but when I focused on her again she seemed to be moving faster. She'd spotted me, and she knew I was following her.

But with luck she *hadn't* spotted George and Bess, and that could make all the difference. . . .

The narrow, cobbled street we were on sloped steeply up a hill lined with shops and restaurants. Another street branched off to the right, with a chain on two squat concrete pillars stretched across it, barring the way. The girl hopped over the chain and started up the hill. I pushed after her.

Because of the chain across it, this street had no vehicle traffic and hardly any pedestrians, either. The girl quickened her pace. I quickened mine, too.

On our right there was a high brick wall, at least twenty feet, with no breaks in it that I could see. On the left there was an alley about twenty-five yards ahead of us. After another glance over her shoulder at me, the girl broke into a run, heading for the alley. Gritting my teeth, I ran after her.

But as she reached it, George stepped out in front of her and grabbed her by the wrist.

"How did you do that?" I demanded as I ran up. "Appear out of nowhere? And where's Bess?"

"Used a live satellite map from my PDA," George said, sounding slightly out of breath. "We ran up the street parallel to this one, figuring we'd be able to cut her off at the alley." She glanced back down the alley. "Bess couldn't keep up. She'll be here in a minute."

I turned to the girl, who was struggling to pull her wrist out of George's grasp. I could have told her that was a lost cause. George is *way* strong.

But I had more pressing concerns on my mind. Like how to say "give me my friend's wallet" in Italian.

I searched my memory for the few words I could remember from the phrase book I'd read on the plane.

"*Um . . . darmi il . . . dinero,*" I said at last. "*Pronto!*"

The girl stared at me, eyes wide. Then . . .

"What did you say?" she asked. In English. With an American accent.

"You're American?" George said, looking surprised. I was startled too. What was an American teenager doing picking pockets in Rome?

At that moment Bess puffed up. "You got her!" she cried. Leaning forward, she rested her hands on her knees while she caught her breath.

"Okay, look," I said to the girl. "I know you've been following us and I know you took my friend's wallet."

"No, I didn't!" the girl protested. "How dare you accuse me!"

I sighed. "I don't want to have to get the police involved, but—"

"No! No police!" she cried, her eyes going even wider.

"Then you'd better give me back my wallet," Bess snapped.

The girl hesitated, as if making up her mind about something. Then, with her free hand she reached into her shoulder bag and pulled out not one wallet, but four.

"Which one?" she asked, sounding defiant.

I gaped at her. "You mean you took all those wallets? Who *are* you?"

Her reaction was completely unexpected. Her chin quivered and her eyes filled with tears. Then she burst out crying.

"I don't know!" she wailed, sobbing. "I don't know who I am!"

CHAPTER **6**

FRANK

THE FIRST SUSPECT

I smiled at the two rottweilers facing me. "Nice doggies," I tried. I wondered if it was true that dogs could smell fear. I hoped not. Although what I was feeling wasn't really what I'd call fear. More like . . . nervousness.

Grrrrrrrrr.

Okay, fine. It was fear.

"Why me?" I muttered. Why was I always the one who had to face the oversize goons or the killer dogs? Why not Joe for a change? He was probably still chatting up that pretty blond girl who was working in his quadrant. He was probably having a fine old time. Unlike me.

Maybe if I acted soothing and gentle I could put the

dogs to sleep. "Good doggie," I said, and held out my hand to the one on the right.

GrrrrrrrrrrrRRRRRR! it replied, its growl getting louder as my hand got closer to it.

Okay. So much for that idea. Time for Plan B: get the heck out of there.

I stepped backward. My foot landed on something wheeled, which promptly started to roll. "Aaaaah!" I couldn't help saying as I began to fall. My arms spun like windmills as I struggled to keep my balance.

It was all the rottweilers needed. Silently, they leaped forward.

I managed to use the fall to my advantage, collapsing to the side so that one dog flew over my head. As it passed over me I reached up and gave it a solid whack in the solar plexus. It hit the concrete floor and lay there, looking stunned.

The other dog was still coming for me, teeth bared. Sending up a silent prayer that this would work, I slammed the heel of my hand straight into its nose. It was something I'd seen on one of those "good animals gone bad" shows on one of the nature channels.

The dog stopped short, and I could swear there was a look of hurt surprise in its eyes. Then, yelping, it turned on its heel and scurried away.

I scrambled up and glanced at the other dog. It had

gotten back on its feet and crouched, glaring at me.

"Oh, yeah?" I said to it. "You wanna mess with me some more? You saw what I just did to your pal there. So tell me, do you feel lucky today?"

In answer, the dog lunged forward, jaws gaping. So much for animal psychology. I turned and ran, leaping over the dolly that had tripped me up before. At the end of the row of palettes I paused to tip a stack of crates into the path behind me. There was a clatter and a yelp.

I didn't stop to inspect the damage. I just kept running toward the light of the loading bay. My backpack bounced on my back. Well, at least if the dog jumped on me from behind it would have to get through the pack first. . . .

I hurdled a low stack of empty palettes and stumbled out into the bright sun.

"What are you doing?" a sharp voice demanded. "Why were you in there?"

Squinting as my eyes adjusted, I turned around. Joanna Paoli stood a few yards away, glaring at me much as the guard dog had. She was carrying a clipboard stacked with shipping forms, and there was a pen tucked behind her ear. I noticed that on her blouse she wore a button with the same design as the flag in the office—a silhouetted head on a white background.

"Sorry," I said, after checking to make sure there was no dog chasing me. "I guess I, uh, went the wrong way.

And then I thought I heard something in the warehouse, so I went to check it out."

"Heard something? Like what?" she shot back.

"Uh—a crashing noise," I said, thinking fast. "Something fell over. I thought maybe there was someone in the warehouse who shouldn't be there."

"You mean, someone like you," Joanna said, folding her arms.

I managed a lame grin. "Yeah, I guess so. I didn't find anyone else in there, anyway. Sorry again."

Without waiting for a response, I turned and headed back in the direction of the train station. But as I walked, I could feel the back of my neck burning.

Was it just embarrassment at how I'd sounded like an idiot in front of a pretty girl? Or was Joanna Paoli's gaze burning a hole in the back of my neck?

I glanced over my shoulder. Sure enough, she stood right where I'd left her, gazing after me.

Hadn't she said she was closing the office? If that clipboard was any indication, she certainly didn't look like she was leaving any time soon. She seemed to be about to take inventory, or whatever it was people did in shipping company warehouses.

So then why had she been so eager to get rid of me?

This trip to the BS&T offices had been a washout, but that didn't mean we were finished with the place. I had the feeling Joanna Paoli had something to hide.

JOE

I laid down my trowel and sat back on my heels, stretching my quads. "Wow," I groaned. "I'm sore. Crouching in the dirt all day turns out to be a work-out!"

Arthur, who was shaking a load full of dust through a sieve next to me, gave me a small, smug grin. "You get used to it," he told me.

"It's just because you're using your muscles in a way they're not used to," Kyra said. She poked my biceps lightly with one finger. "But you're in good shape, you'll adjust fast."

Arthur's smile disappeared and he looked gloomy. I guess Kyra never touched *his* biceps and told him he was in good shape.

I glanced at my watch. "Quitting time," I said with a sigh of relief. "So what's everyone doing tonight? Going out on the town?"

"You'll be too tired to party the night away, I promise you that. But there's a restaurant where a lot of us usually meet up for dinner," Kyra said.

"It's a real hole in the wall," Arthur threw in. "You probably wouldn't like it."

Kyra gave him a puzzled look, then turned back to me. "It's not fancy, but it's very homey. It's a little place near the university that serves good spaghetti and great homemade bread for not much money. You and your brother should meet us there."

"Sounds great. What time?" I said. Clearly Arthur would prefer it if I didn't show up, but I wasn't going to let that stop me. Yes, Frank and I were in Rome on a mission, but even secret agents have to eat. We might as well try to have a good time, too.

"We meet around eight," Kyra said. "I know that sounds late, but in Rome most people don't actually eat dinner till more like nine or ten. The restaurant is always empty when we arrive. It fills up, though."

"Cool," I said. "I'm sure Frank will be into it. All right, I'm going to go hook up with him now. I'll see you two later."

Stepping over the string boundary of our quadrant, I stopped to stretch one more time. Then I walked over to Frank's quadrant. I was eager to fill him in on my suspicions about Vanessa.

He wasn't there. In fact, no one was there. The quadrant was deserted, and from the way it had been tidied up, I guessed that all the workers had left for the day already. I walked around the dig site, but I didn't see Frank anywhere.

I frowned. It wasn't like him to slack off. It also wasn't like him to disappear without telling me where he was going. In fact, if I was being honest, both those traits sounded more like me than like my brother.

Well, I thought, *just because he's slacking off doesn't mean I should. I'm going to follow up my lead on my own.* And then when my brother and I finally did catch up with each other, with any luck I'd have something to report.

I strolled over to Vanessa's office, which was in one of the two trailers that sat at the edge of the dig site. Glancing around, I made sure that no one was watching. Then, still moving casually, I reached for the doorknob.

It was locked. Not really a surprise, and not much of a complication, either, since the doorknob was one of those cheap models that you can buy in any hardware store. Easy as pie. I pulled out my pocket knife and selected the toothpick. Sliding it into the lock, I jiggled it around until I felt the tumblers inside click.

And that was that. I was in. Checking once more to make sure I wasn't being observed, I slipped inside the trailer.

"Whew, what a mess," I muttered as I looked around. The blinds were pulled down and the small room was in shadow. A desk and chair stood against one wall, a long metal table opposite them. Books and papers were stacked on every surface, including the floor. There was an electric kettle on the table, with dirty mugs littered around it. The entire place smelled of overcooked coffee.

It wouldn't be easy finding clues in this mess. But I was going to give it my best shot.

Moving to the desk, I picked up one of the stacks of paper and scanned it. It was a color photocopy of some pages from a book about Roman coins. Scrawled notes in the margins said things like "C. 250? AF at UR to verify," and "Note variations in head position. Within expected pars?" I didn't know what any of it meant, but I was fairly sure that it all had something to do with archaeology. Whatever these pages were, they seemed to be a legitimate part of the dig.

Well, I'd barely even scratched the surface. Shifting that stack aside, I poked through the other books and papers on the desk top. But it was all boringly legitimate. No suspicious IOUs, no betting slips or giant credit card bills. Nor, for that matter, any artifacts. They must all be in the cataloging trailer, which was where they were supposed to be. All I could see here was more and more stuff about cruddy old clay pots and moldy old medallions.

I shifted my stance and accidentally knocked over a teetering pile of books on the table behind me. Some of them slid off the table top and onto the floor, making a louder noise than I liked. I froze for an instant, but no one seemed to be coming in to check, so I got on with my search. I'd better move faster, just to be on the safe side. It could be awkward if anyone found me in here.

Then, partially buried under a drift of papers on the desk chair, I spotted an olive-green leather satchel. Vanessa's purse! I'd noticed her carrying it that morning when she arrived at the dig site.

If there were going to be any useful clues to the source of her money problems, they were likely to be in her purse. I picked it up and undid the buckles that held the main flap closed.

I peered inside. The bag was full of crumpled bits of paper and odds and ends, every bit as messy as Vanessa's office. I also spotted a wallet . . . hairbrush . . . zippered vinyl bag that I guessed was a makeup case. . . .

Suddenly the door swung open and daylight streamed in, slanting across the desk. I looked up, blinking. Vanessa stood silhouetted in the doorway. I couldn't make out her face, but her voice when it came out was an angry squeak.

"Just what do you think you're doing, pawing through my things?" she demanded. Stepping inside, she slammed the door behind her. "You've got some explaining to do!"

Whoops. This was, to say the least, awkward!

I stepped around the far side of the desk, Vanessa's purse still dangling from my hands. I was going to tell her I'd found it somewhere on the dig site and was just returning it to her. Lame, I know, but it might have worked.

As it turned out, though, I never did find out whether it would have worked. As I stepped forward, my toe caught on the edge of a wooden packing crate I hadn't noticed before. The lid, which hadn't been fastened down, slid to one side. I glanced down and saw a welter of foam packing peanuts.

And, sticking out of the peanuts, two ancient-looking pottery vases.

I knew enough about dig procedure to know that there was something wrong here. The artifacts were supposed to be catalogued and stored under very strict conditions, not held in someone's office in a packing crate.

Frowning, I bent down and took a look at the address on the crate lid.

Sr. Antonio Petrelli, Mercato delle Stampe, V. Beccaria 17, Roma.

Now, I happened to know that the Mercato delle Stampe was a big open-air antiques market held at the Piazza del Popolo. I knew this because one of the people who'd briefed me and Frank was a woman who had a stall there who was an authority on ancient artifacts. She was also a spy attached to the American Embassy.

Why would Vanessa be sending ancient pottery from the dig to an antiques market? There was no reason I could think of—no legitimate reason, anyway.

I glanced up at her. She was frozen in place, her face white and scared. The picture of guilt. I shook my head.

"No, Vanessa," I said. "I think you're the one with explaining to do."

CHAPTER 7

NANCY

LILY DOE

The girl who had stolen Bess's wallet stood on the cobblestone street, sobbing as if her heart were broken. Bess, George, and I all stood around her in a semicircle. I felt at a loss for what to do. This was so not what I'd expected!

"Do you think she's faking it?" Bess whispered. "You know, trying to get us to feel so sorry for her that we'll let her go?"

George shrugged. "If she is, she deserves an Academy Award."

"Yeah," I agreed, studying the girl. "I think whatever is wrong with her, it's real. At least, real to her."

After a few minutes the girl's sobs began to grow less violent. I stepped forward and took her arm gently.

Rummaging in my pocket, I came up with a crumpled but clean tissue and handed it to her. "What do you mean, you don't know who you are?" I asked. "Can you tell me your name?"

The girl dabbed her eyes and gulped. "No," she said in a muffled voice. "I . . . I can't remember it."

Over her head, I exchanged glances with Bess and George. "What can you remember?" I asked.

"N-n-nothing!" the girl said, and burst out crying again.

Oh, boy. This was a very strange twist in our day!

"Let's go sit down," Bess suggested, and led us back down the little alley to a restaurant at the other end that had a few tables set up outside. We took seats and an impassive waiter brought us a bottle of water and four glasses.

George poured the girl some water and handed it to her. She sipped, calming down slowly.

Finally she looked around at us through reddened eyes. "I can't remember anything before yesterday morning," she said in a small voice.

"Okay, let's start there. Where were you, and what were you doing, yesterday morning?" I asked.

"I was having a horrible nightmare—that I was locked up someplace small and pitch dark and damp and smelly, and that I knew someone was coming to kill me. Then I woke up, and I was on a bench in a big park of some kind. I think it's called the Borghese gardens—that's what a tourist told me. I woke up, and I had no idea what I was doing there, or how I got there."

The girl's face started to crumple again, and to head off a renewed bout of sobs, I asked, "Do you think you slept there all night?"

"I must have. I was all stiff and my hair was flat on one side from lying on the bench. I had a hairbrush in my bag, and I washed my face and cleaned up in the public restrooms up there in the park," the girl told us. "Then I went back and just sat there for a while, on that bench where I'd slept. I guess I hoped that if I stayed there long enough, someone would come find me. You know, someone would be looking for me." At this she did start to cry again.

"I'm sure someone *is* looking for you," Bess said in a gentle voice. "Your family and friends will find you soon. Don't worry."

"I don't know," the girl said, biting her lip. "What if they don't know I'm in Rome? I mean, what am I doing here? How did I get here? I know I don't live here—that much I'm sure of."

"What about the American Embassy?" I suggested. "You've got to be American, or possibly Canadian, from the way you speak English. You can go to the embassies and find out if they've been asked to look for any missing travelers."

"Oh." The girl looked startled, as if the idea of official help had never even occurred to her. And, in fairness, I had to admit, why would it? She had enough to worry about, being alone in a strange city with no memory.

"So what did you do between then and now?" George wanted to know. "How have you spent the last two days?"

"Walking around," the girl said. "Trying to get some money so I can get a place to stay."

"Get some money? You mean, by stealing people's wallets?" Bess's tone grew chilly.

The girl shrugged. "I don't know why, but I'm good at it," she said with a trace of pride. "You're the first one who even noticed me, and that was only because someone jostled me right when I was reaching into your bag. Otherwise you'd never have caught me."

"It's true," I had to agree. "I noticed you a few times during the day, but I just assumed you were another tourist and it was a coincidence you were in the same places we were. But it wasn't a coincidence—you had marked us, hadn't you?"

"Just her," the girl said, gesturing at Bess with her chin. "She looked like a good possibility, with that shoulder bag. I wouldn't have tried it with either of you two." She glanced from George to me.

George grinned. Bess's eyes narrowed. "Hmmm," she sniffed.

I checked my watch. "Guys, we should get going pretty soon if we're going to make it back to the pensione by seven," I said.

The girl looked panicked. "You're going to leave me? You can't!"

I hesitated. There was something about this girl that I didn't quite like. Maybe it was the fact that she didn't seem to feel the least bit guilty about stealing all those people's wallets.

On the other hand, she *was* in a very tough spot. Maybe I shouldn't judge her so harshly. And it was true, we couldn't just abandon her, helpless as she was. There was no way I'd be able to live with myself if I did that.

"George, can you find the US Embassy on your PDA?" I asked. "We can take, um—" I broke off. "I don't know what to call you," I told the girl. "For now, why don't you just pick a name you like—that is, until your real name comes back to you."

The girl pursed her lips as she thought. "Lily is a pretty name," she said after a moment. "Yeah, call me Lily."

"All right then, Lily it is." We all introduced ourselves.

"As I was saying," I resumed, "we can take Lily to the embassy on our way back to the pensione."

"It's not exactly on our way," George said, after consulting her PDA. "In fact, it's in almost the opposite direction, northeast of where we are now. But it's not far. We can walk there in fifteen minutes or so. It's on Via Vittorio Veneto."

Bess bit her lip. "Okay, but we better not be late," she said. "Aunt Estelle hates it when people are late. And we have no way to call her and tell her—there's no phone in the pensione."

"We'll take a cab back," I promised. "Let's go."

I paid for the water and we headed out, George leading the way. We crossed Via della Panetteria (which I was pretty sure meant street of the bakeries, though I didn't see any bakeries on it) and walked up a small street called Via in Arcione, which led us to the major avenue called Via del Tritone.

As we were turning right onto Via del Tritone, a scooter zipped past us and let out a loud backfire. Lily gave a little gasp. I glanced at her.

She looked as if she were about to faint. She put out a hand to steady herself on a street sign.

"What's wrong?" I asked.

She shook her head. "That sound. It just—it scared me, that's all."

I studied her discreetly as we resumed walking. Now that I was looking, I noticed that she flinched every time a car passed. What could have happened to her? How had she lost her memory? I was beginning to suspect that she'd been through something pretty traumatic. Her reactions to loud noises clearly pointed in that direction.

Should we be taking her to a hospital instead of to the embassy? I wondered. Maybe she needed medical help.

"Left here," George instructed, and we turned up a broad, curving, tree-lined street marked Via Vittorio Veneto. Well, I figured, we were almost there. Might as well stick to the original plan.

But when we arrived at the US Embassy, things got a bit more complicated.

"There it is!" Bess said, pointing at an imposing salmon-colored building across the street from us. It was surrounded by a high stone wall, and guards in army uniforms stood on either side of the gate. "Let's go."

"Wait!" Lily cried suddenly.

We all turned and looked at her. She was standing as though she were glued to the sidewalk. Her face was white, her eyes huge. "I can't go in there," she said in a faint voice.

"What do you mean?" George asked.

"Why?" Bess added.

"I can't. I just can't," Lily repeated. Her chest heaved as if she was having trouble breathing.

"It'll be okay," I told her. "We'll all go with you. I promise nothing bad will happen to you. Come on, all you have to do is cross the street and walk through the gate."

Lily shook her head violently. "I can't!" she said again. I heard real terror in her voice. Then she turned and began to walk rapidly down the street the way we'd come. Her steps quickened until she was almost running.

"Oh, for goodness' sake," George muttered, sounding exasperated. She checked her watch again. "We don't have time for this!"

"Wait here," I told my friends. I ran after Lily, catching up with her about halfway to the next corner. When I touched her shoulder, she jumped almost a foot in the air.

"It's just me," I told her. "What happened back there? What was so scary about the embassy?"

"It was those men," Lily said. She gazed at me with wide eyes. "The ones by the gate. I thought they were going to hurt me."

"They're just guards," I told her. "They won't hurt you." I took a deep breath. "Lily, I think you need medical help. Something scary happened to you, and you blocked it out, but now you need a doctor or psychiatrist who can help you get your memories back. I have to go home now, but let me put you in a taxi to the nearest hospital. I'll come tomorrow and see how you're doing, I promise."

"No!" Lily seized my arm in a grip so tight that I winced. "You can't leave me! You can't do that to me. You're my only friends!"

I resisted the urge to point out that (a) *she'd* just walked away from *us* and (b) we weren't her friends. We'd only just met, and we wouldn't have met if she hadn't been robbing Bess.

Bess and George walked up. "Nan, we really have to go," Bess said. "We're already late for Aunt Estelle as it is. If we don't go now, we'll even be late for dinner."

I shrugged my shoulders in surrender. "Guys, I don't know what to do," I admitted. "We can't just leave Lily here. The only thing I can think of is to take her back to the pensione with us."

"There is room," Bess said slowly. The pensione had three bedrooms.

"There's also Aunt Estelle," George pointed out. Then she sighed. "But you're right, Nancy. We don't have a choice. I just hope Aunt Estelle doesn't mind another teenage girl around the place."

"Oh, thank you, thank you! I promise I won't be any trouble," Lily cried. Her face lit up. "I knew you'd help me. I knew you wouldn't let me down!"

Bess looked at me. "*I* knew a vacation with no mysteries to solve couldn't really happen," she said with a wry smile. "Not when Nancy Drew, detective, is around."

"You're a *detective*?" Lily squealed. "Well then, it's fate! You can find out who I am and where I belong!" She beamed at me as if she'd just done me a huge favor.

I couldn't help laughing. The whole situation was just so bizarre!

Though I'd never dreamed it could happen on a trip to Rome, and I hadn't been searching for one, a mystery had found me.

It looked like I was starting my newest case!

CHAPTER **8**

JOE

CASE CLOSED?

Vanessa stared at me across the cluttered office. Shock and anger warred with each other in her face, and I knew that if I wanted to control the situation I'd have to keep up my offensive.

I pointed to the crate with the vases. "You want to tell me what these are doing here?" I demanded. "Or should we take it to the university sponsors and you can explain to them?" I started to lift the crate. "In fact, I think that's what we should do. It would be the proper protocol, wouldn't it?"

"No!" Vanessa burst out, and I knew I had her.

I straightened up and faced her, folding my arms. "All right then, maybe you can explain it to me," I said.

"Who are you?" Vanessa asked in a trembling voice.

"I *knew* there was something funny about you and your brother just turning up here without anyone knowing where you'd come from. And you obviously know nothing about archaeology."

I was hurt. I thought I'd been doing a great job of sifting dirt!

"Were you sent here to check up on me?" Vanessa asked.

I realized I had to tread carefully here. If I said too much, she might realize how little I actually knew. But I had to convince her that I was the voice of authority, so she'd tell me the truth.

"We were sent here, yes," I said. "We're working with the Italian authorities." Then I frowned. "But I'm not here to answer questions, I'm here to ask them. So tell me, who's this Petrelli guy? How does the scam work? How do you get the pots off site without anyone noticing that they're missing?"

Vanessa looked bewildered. "Are you talking about these pots here? Why would anyone notice they're missing?" she asked. "They're not from the dig."

I blinked. "You mean you're stealing from other digs as well?"

"Stealing?" Vanessa looked even more confused. "Of course not! I would never steal artifacts from a dig! That would be a . . . a violation of history!"

"Well, if you're not stealing, then how do you explain

these pots?" I asked. I was starting to get annoyed. Did she think I was that stupid, that I'd believe her denials with the evidence right there at my feet?

"You mean you don't . . . oh, my goodness!" Vanessa exclaimed. She put her hand over her mouth. "*You* thought I'd been nicking things from the dig and selling them. And *I* thought you were after me for the knockoffs!"

I must have had a bewildered look myself now, because she glanced at me and explained, "The pots in that crate are fakes. Knockoffs. I'm a potter, and I'm also an archaeologist, so I know how to make the pots the way the Romans did, and then how to make them look properly aged, so that people think they're actual antiques.

"It's not illegal," she went on quickly as I opened my mouth. "At least, not my part of it. I never claimed they were anything but historically accurate copies."

"But the antique dealers you sell them to are reselling them as the real thing," I guessed.

"I don't know that for a fact," Vanessa argued, looking uncomfortable.

"You suspect, though, don't you?"

She sagged. "Please, you don't have to tell anyone here, do you? It's not illegal, but it *is* a bit . . . well, unsavory. It won't do my career any good."

I perched on the edge of her desk. "I don't know yet

whether I can keep you out of it," I said. "We're working on a bigger investigation. Obviously I can't give you details on that, but I think it's safe to say we're not after you. I can try to keep your part of things quiet, but I'm going to need your cooperation."

Vanessa nodded eagerly. "Anything," she said. "Tell me how I can help."

"First of all, tell me more about this scam of yours." She winced when I used the word *scam*, but I went on. "How long have you been doing it, and why? Why jeopardize your career by making forgeries?"

"It's my younger brother," Vanessa said sadly. "Anthony. I've always been sort of a mother to him— our mum died when he was just a kid—and I suppose he's a bit dependent on me. He's also addicted to gambling. He had a bad losing streak a while back and apparently he borrowed money from a gangster, a loan shark, to pay it off." She sighed. "And now, of course, everything is ten times worse. The loan shark wants his money back, plus an outrageous amount of interest, and Tony can't pay it, and the sum keeps getting bigger every day, and now Tony is afraid he's going to be killed."

I shook my head. How did people get themselves into these crazy messes?

"He phoned me a month ago, frightened out of his mind," Vanessa went on. "I sent him all the money I had, but a week later he needed more. The only thing I could think of to make a lot of money quickly was to do this." She waved at the pots. "They pay me two hundred Euro apiece for them. I can make about four a week, if I work on them every night. It's quite an involved process, see, with a lot of steps to it."

Two hundred Euro times four? "So you're making eight hundred Euro a week on these pots?" I said, impressed. "Over a thousand dollars. That's not bad!"

"It all depends how you look at it," Vanessa retorted. "I look at it as meaning I'll have to keep doing it for months to pay off Tony's debt. And it's worn me out. I'm up all night every night making the pots, and then I'm here all day every day."

"That's why you've been so irritable," I guessed.

Vanessa let out a short laugh. "Have I? Sorry about that. I didn't notice. I've been so worried, I haven't really been paying attention to the dig at all."

"So when you get phone calls at the dig, is that mostly your brother calling you?" I wanted to know.

"Sometimes it's Tony," Vanessa said. "I also have to make a lot of arrangements with the various dealers I sell to. It takes time." She moved to the long table and gathered together the dirty coffee mugs, staring at them blankly. "And today the man Tony owes the money to rang me. I suppose Tony must have told him where the payments were coming from. He told me I needed to pay faster." Her chin wobbled. "How can I do that? I can't possibly work any harder or faster than I am now."

"Can't Tony pitch in?" I asked.

She shook her head. "He's in college. He's got to keep up with his studies."

Tony sounded like a bit of a jerk, I thought but didn't say. He had enough time to pile up a massive gambling debt, but not enough time to help his sister get him out of the mess he'd made?

Still, that wasn't really the point right now. "Look, let me talk to the people I work with," I said. "We might be able to help you out. Do you know the name of this loan shark your brother borrowed from?"

Vanessa's hand went to the frame of her rectangular glasses and she adjusted them nervously. "Won't that put Tony in danger, if I give this man's name to the police?"

"We'll be very discreet," I assured her.

She bit her lip. "It's a man called Fat Hamish—I don't know his surname. He's in London."

"Okay," I said, nodding. "Tonight I'll talk to the people I work with and see if they can't find some way to get this Fat Hamish character to back off.

"Now, I need you to help me, if you can. You remember Sam Lewis, the kid who got arrested for try-ing to sell those artifacts?"

"Of course," Vanessa said. She carried the dirty mugs over to the tiny sink in the corner and began scrubbing them. My promise of help seemed to have given her new energy. "He was a good worker," she said over her shoulder, "and he seemed very serious about archaeology. I was surprised when he stopped showing up. I assumed that girlfriend of his must have had something to do with it. Caitlin. I didn't care for her—she was forever distracting him, trying to get him to leave work and spend time with her. I was ever so shocked when I heard about him getting arrested, though. He never struck me as the criminal type."

"Any idea how he got hold of the artifacts that he tried to sell?" I asked.

Vanessa carried the clean mugs back to the table and began scooping paper into piles. "Ugh, this place is such a mess. On the next rainy day, I've got to get in here and sort out all the paperwork," she muttered. In a louder voice, she added, "I don't know for a fact how he got hold of them, but I assume it must have been once they were at the BS and T warehouse. When I heard about the case, I checked our catalog and all those artifacts he tried to sell were listed as having been sent out to BS and T already. But, of course, taking them from BS and T would have been dead easy for Sam."

I looked at Vanessa in surprise. "Why do you say that?"

"Well, because Caitlin worked there, of course,"

Vanessa said. She arched her eyebrows at me. "Didn't you know?"

I think my jaw actually dropped. We hadn't known that, and it seemed like a big oversight!

"Yes, Sam told me he'd gotten her a job there. I think it must have been off the books, since she didn't have authorization to work in Italy," Vanessa added. "They needed some extra help in the office. Filing, that sort of thing."

That explained it. ATAC would have access to only the official list of employees from BS&T. If Caitlin had been working there illegally, there would have been no record of it—and no way for ATAC to know.

I rubbed my chin thoughtfully. It now seemed clear to me how the theft had worked. Caitlin had stolen the things from BS&T and then given them to Sam to sell. Which meant that, more than likely, there was no theft ring or conspiracy at the dig. We were barking up the wrong tree. Of course Frank and I would have to confirm this, but it seemed that our investigation was pretty much over.

A grin broke over my face. Wait till I told my big brother I'd cracked the case on my own! And that this time there would be no masked goons or other assorted thugs to deal with. He'd be so happy!

Speaking of Frank, I wondered again where he'd gotten to.

"All right, Vanessa, you've helped with this investigation, and I appreciate it," I told her. "We'll see what we can do to get your brother off the hook with Fat Hamish—I'll get back to you in a couple of days with something more concrete. And don't worry, I think I can promise that we won't need to reveal what you've been doing on the side."

"Thanks very much. Oh, it's such a relief to have someone to turn to!" Vanessa said. Now that her secret was out in the open she seemed like a different person— friendly, helpful, basically pretty nice. "I'd give anything to be able to stop making these knockoff pots. And I will, as soon as I know that Tony's safe."

Nodding to her, I left the trailer. As soon as I was outside, I pulled out my phone to call Frank.

The phone was switched off. I must have forgotten to turn it on that morning. Which meant that maybe Frank *had* tried to reach me to let me know where he was going. Whoops. . . .

Whatever. I switched it on and hit Frank's speed-dial number.

"Where have you been?" was my brother's greeting to me. "I've been trying to call you for hours! Did you get my text?"

"Sorry, phone was turned off," I told him. "But—"

"I'm going to lose the connection in a second. I'm on a train going into a tunnel," he cut me off. "Meet me back at our room and we'll talk. I've got a few leads."

"I've got more than—," I started to say. But then I realized I was speaking into a dead phone. My big brother had hung up on me.

FRANK

Joe reached our dorm about fifteen minutes after me. I'd been pacing the room, waiting for him. "Man, you would not believe the day I've had," I burst out as soon as he walked in the door. "Do you know that I was attacked by two rottweilers? Not one, but two. And I whacked my shin really hard, too." And made a fool of myself in front of a pretty girl, I almost added. But that was too embarrassing to talk about.

"Whoa, whoa, slow down, brother," Joe said, raising his hands. "Where were you attacked by rottweilers? What were you doing?"

"Didn't you even look at the text I sent you?" I asked. "I went to the BS and T offices."

"Really? Now that's a coincidence," Joe said. A funny little smile crossed his face. "Go on."

"Why is it a coincidence?" I asked.

"No, no, I'll tell you my news after you tell me yours," Joe said, waving a hand. His smile got wider.

"Whatever," I grumbled. After the day I'd had, I was

feeling pretty irritable. If Joe wanted to act mysterious, let him.

I told him about my trip, Joanna Paoli's suspicious behavior, and my encounter with the dogs. "It's not much to go on, but I just have a hunch there's a connection at BS and T," I finished. "I think we need to focus our investigation there."

"I agree that BS and T is key," Joe said. "But I think the investigation is pretty much over." His smile became a broad, triumphant grin. "I cracked the case this afternoon, bro. All by my little self."

"What?" I stared at him.

"There is no theft ring," Joe said. "At least, not one involving the people here at the dig. Sam's girlfriend Caitlin is the key. She worked at BS and T, and I'm sure she's the one who stole the artifacts that Sam tried to sell."

"How do you know this?" I demanded, flabbergasted.

"Long story, which I'll go into later. The short version is that I got Vanessa to open up," Joe said airily. "Apparently Sam got Caitlin a job at BS and T, working off the books—which, by the way, is why ATAC didn't know about it. She was in a perfect position to steal stuff from their warehouse. And from what I've heard, she was sort of a shifty character."

"Yeah," I said slowly. "I heard the same thing. Wow,

this does put a whole new spin on things, doesn't it? Nice work, Joe."

"Thank you, thank you." Joe made a little bow. "And sorry about your run-in with the rottweilers. I was hoping we could get out of this mission without any mauling at all, but I guess these days no case is complete unless big bro gets himself in trouble. Remember when it used to be the other way around?"

"Don't remind me," I groaned.

"The good old days," Joe said in a mock-wistful voice.

"You know, it's not quite over yet," I said after a moment. "We now have a pretty good idea of how Sam got hold of those artifacts, but we still need to try to find actual evidence. Best thing would be if we could track down this Caitlin girl herself."

"Right. And if that means we have to stay in Rome a few extra days . . . well, I guess we'll just have to grin and bear it," Joe put in with a laugh.

I ignored that. "I'm going to e-mail ATAC and see what they can dig up on Caitlin. The other thing is, before we close the book for sure on the idea of a theft ring, I'd like to nose around some more about those Emerald-Eyed Lions that everyone seems to think should have been dug up by now."

"I forgot about those." Joe walked over to a chair and flung himself down. "Do you really think there's a crime there? I mean, couldn't those things have been dug up hundreds of years ago? Or maybe the emperor Claudius or whoever had them moved, way back when. Maybe he decided they'd look better in one of his other houses."

"You're probably right," I agreed. "I'd just like to do a little more investigating before we give up.

"You know," I added as a thought struck me, "Nancy and her friends might be able to help us find Caitlin. We can ask tomorrow when we see them, anyway."

"I like the way you think," Joe said. "And I'm sure your making that suggestion has nothing to do with you having a crush on Nancy, does it?"

"Shut up," I growled, and whacked Joe in the side of the head. "I just think it would help to have a few extra people if there's a lot of legwork to do."

"Uh-huh, whatever you say," Joe murmured with an annoying twinkle in his eye. "Okay, so what's on our to-do list?"

"I'll e-mail ATAC now," I said. "Then, tomorrow, we need to go back to BS and T and see if we can find out more about Caitlin. By which I mean *you* need to go to BS and T. I can't go there—that girl Joanna is already suspicious of me." I frowned. "It looks like there's not much point in our continuing to work on the dig. I hope Vanessa isn't too upset to lose us."

"Don't worry, I can make it right with her," Joe said. "By the way, I promised her I'd call in a favor with ATAC for her. Wait till I tell you *her* story. . . ."

I listened to what he had to say as I booted up my computer. I had to admit, my little bro had done some good work today, even if I hadn't.

Yes, I thought, even though it had involved rottweilers, this was one of our easier and more fun assignments. Too bad it seemed like it was ending already. I hoped ATAC would at least let us hang out a few days and take in some of the sights. It seemed like not much to ask, after we'd completed our mission in record time.

Little did I know, this case was far from closed. . . .

CHAPTER **9**

NANCY

LILY OF THE VALLEY

By bedtime I was wondering if I'd made a huge mistake.

The trouble had begun almost as soon as we got home. Aunt Estelle had welcomed Lily with her trademark graciousness and generosity. "I'm sure we can fit another place in at dinner," she'd said. "Ugo will be delighted to add another pretty face to his table."

Lily had tugged my arm. "I don't want to go out," she'd whispered to me. Her lips trembled. "I'm scared, I'm tired, I want to take a bath. Can't we just stay here tonight?"

I'd been looking forward to this dinner ever since Aunt Estelle had told us about it. Her friend Ugo Artom came from a wealthy old family, and he apparently lived in some sort of castle just outside Rome, filled with art and antiques and clanking suits of armor. (The pensione we were staying in was just an extra apartment he used when he had business that kept him overnight in the city.) I'd never met anyone who lived in a castle before! And Aunt Estelle said his dinner parties were legendary.

But Lily was so frail, so vulnerable. It wasn't right to drag her out after all she'd been through. And it wouldn't be right to leave her here on her own, either.

I swallowed my disappointment. "Aunt Estelle, I'm really sorry to do this," I said. "But I think Lily needs a quiet evening. I'm happy to stay here with her while you all go to Mr. Artom's party. Please give him my best and tell him I hope I can visit another time."

Aunt Estelle pursed her lips. "All right," she said after a moment. "I suppose you're right."

But once Aunt Estelle, Bess, and George were gone, Lily didn't settle down the way I thought she would. She prowled from room to room of the big old apartment, picking things up, fingering things.

"Man, this guy must be really rich if this is his spare apartment," she said. She pointed to a small, dim charcoal drawing of a woman's face that hung on the wall in the foyer. "That's a sketch for Tiepolo's *Meeting of Anthony and Cleopatra*. And I think it's real."

"Wow," I said, impressed. Then something else hit

me. "Hey, how did you know all that?" I asked. "About the drawing."

Lily shrugged. "I don't know. Why does it matter?"

"It tells us something about you," I told her. I drummed my fingers on a tabletop. "Maybe you're an artist, or an art history student."

"Hmmm." Lily cocked her head to one side as she thought about that. "Maybe I am." She sighed. "I thought if I figured out something about me that was true, really true, you know, it would sort of click into place and I'd be like, *Oh yeah, that's right!* But I'm not getting that feeling."

"It might not work that way," I told her gently. "I don't know much about amnesia, but it might just be that your memories need time to rebuild themselves." Seeing an opening, I went on. "You know, I really do think we should take you to a doctor tomorrow. Medicine might be able to help you in ways that I can't."

"We'll see," Lily said in a vague way, and started prowling again. I had the feeling she was trying to avoid the subject.

Suddenly she turned to me. "Hey, you want to get out of here? I feel sort of restless."

I stared at her in puzzlement. "Lily, you just told me all you wanted to do is stay in and take a bath. If you wanted to go out, we should have gone to Mr. Artom's dinner party."

"Oh, that sounded so stuffy," Lily said, waving her hand. "Who wants to spend the evening with a bunch of old people?" She must have seen my expression, because she quickly added, "I mean, I really did feel exhausted, and I do want to take a bath, but I'm starting to get some energy back. I think it's because I'm not scared right now. I feel safe with you." She offered me a smile.

But this time I wasn't buying her routine. "I really wanted to go to that dinner party," I told her. "I'd been looking forward to it all day. I stayed here because I thought you needed it. And now I find out you just thought you could come up with something better to do?"

"I'm sorry," Lily said in a pathetic little voice. "Don't be mad at me."

I pressed my lips together to avoid letting out an angry retort. Turning, I walked into the living room and stood by the window, gazing out at the cityscape while I struggled with my exasperation.

After a minute or two I'd cooled down. "Why don't you go take that bath," I suggested to Lily. "I'll put together some dinner for us—I'm starving, aren't you? There are a few things in the kitchen."

"Okay." Lily padded off toward the bathroom while I went into the kitchen. I heard the water start to run into the tub.

Rummaging through the fridge produced some excellent results. Aunt Estelle, who was a good cook, had made a great Bolognese sauce a couple of nights before, full of meat and vegetables simmered in a tomato-cream sauce, and there was plenty left over. It just needed reheating. I put some water on to boil for pasta and threw together some salad greens and sliced tomatoes. There was a hunk of goat cheese in the fridge, so I added that to the salad, too. I set the salad bowl on the table with oil and vinegar. I was enjoying myself. At home I sometimes help our housekeeper, Hannah Gruen, in the kitchen, but I don't often put together a meal by myself.

While I waited for the water to boil, I went back into the living room and popped one of my favorite CDs into the player. Humming along under my breath, I sat down and picked up a fold-out map of Rome that was sitting on the coffee table. I found the Villa Borghese gardens and studied the area around them, trying to see if there was anything that would help me get some idea of what had happened to Lily.

I'd been thinking about what she said at the very beginning, about that nightmare she had right before she woke up in the park. Of course, it could have been just a coincidental bad dream, but what if it wasn't? What if she really had been locked up somewhere dark and damp and smelly? Was there any place like that near the Borghese gardens?

I shook my head in frustration. The map was a tourist map. It couldn't tell me anything useful, like where the bad neighborhoods were or if there were underground caves anywhere.

I wondered if there was any way I could jog Lily's memory. It could be dangerous, I knew, to try to make an amnesia victim remember painful events. The results were impossible to predict. But maybe we could talk after dinner, when she was a little more relaxed and felt more secure.

I went into the kitchen and checked the pasta water. It was boiling, so I added a handful of linguine.

I crossed to the bathroom and knocked on the door. "Dinner will be ready in a few minutes. How's the bath going?" I called.

No answer. "Lily?" I called. When there was still no answer, I opened the door a crack and peeked in.

The tub was full of water, and the air was full of steam, but Lily wasn't in there.

My heart thudded. I had instantaneous visions of mysterious men in black kidnapping her from the tub. Where was she? What could have happened to her?

I spun around—and let out a yelp of surprise. Lily was standing in the doorway of Bess and George's room, wearing a pink terrycloth robe and a towel around her hair.

"You scared me to death! I didn't know where you

were," I said, taking a deep breath to get my pulse under control. "What are you doing in Bess and George's room? You're sharing a room with me, remember?"

"I got confused about which one it was," Lily said, shrugging. "Went into the wrong one."

I frowned as I recognized the robe. "Isn't that Bess's robe?"

"Is it?" Lily glanced down at it. "It was hanging in the bathroom, so I just put it on. You don't think she'll mind if I borrow it, do you?"

"I guess not," I said, somewhat absently. I was thinking, *I don't remember seeing Bess's robe hanging in the bathroom today.* In fact, I specifically remembered seeing it lying across her bed when I'd gone in there to borrow some hand cream just before they all left for dinner.

Lily was lying. I wasn't sure why—maybe it wasn't the most polite thing to do, but it wasn't a crime for her to go into Bess's room and borrow her robe. But the fact that she had lied about it set off alarm bells in my head. Lily was a thief. Had she taken anything?

While she went into our room to get dressed, I popped into Bess and George's room and quickly scanned the dressers and tabletops. I didn't notice anything obviously out of place, but that didn't comfort me all that much. There was no way for me to tell if anything was missing. I made a mental note to tell Bess and George to check over their belongings later.

When Lily came to the table to eat, she looked at the bowl of linguine I'd set out for her and made a face. "Does that have meat in it?" she asked.

"Yes, it does," I said, trying not to get annoyed again by the accusing note in her voice. "Why?"

"I'm vegetarian," Lily stated. "Meat is murder."

Okay. . . .

"I'm sorry. I didn't know," I told her. "But I'm glad you remembered that about yourself. Maybe it's a sign your memory is coming back."

"Maybe. But in the meantime, what am I going to eat?" she asked plaintively. "I'm *starving*."

I took a deep breath. *Calm down*, I told myself. *Remember, she's in a very stressful situation. I'm sure she doesn't mean to be rude.*

"I could make you some plain pasta with olive oil and cheese," I offered.

"Okay," she said without much enthusiasm.

I did that, which took another twenty minutes. By the time we sat down to eat, my linguine Bolognese was stone cold. I watched with my jaw clenched as Lily ate a few bites of pasta, picked the tomatoes out of her salad and lined them up on the edge of her plate, nibbled a lettuce leaf, and then pushed the whole plate aside.

"I guess I'm not as hungry as I thought," she said with a little laugh. She leaned back and gave a huge yawn. "Wow, I am completely exhausted. Would you mind very much if I left the cleanup to you? I'd love to help, but after what I've been through I think I just really need to get some sleep."

I could barely summon the will to nod. Whatever else Lily was, she was clearly a first-class user!

I took my time cleaning up the kitchen, trying to work off the irritation I was feeling. Scrubbing pots made me feel better. By the time I was done, Lily was in the bedroom we were sharing with the door closed. There was no light coming from the crack at the bottom.

I sat down in the living room to read and wait for my other friends to come home. I hoped their evening had been as pleasant as mine had been annoying.

They came in just before midnight. George was describing the incredible castle and the fabulous meal when Bess came out of their shared bedroom. "Has anyone seen my oatmeal cleansing milk?" she asked. "I left it on the bureau this morning but now it's not there. Nan, did you borrow it?"

I shook my head. "Not me." Then I remembered. "Um—maybe Lily did. I know she borrowed your robe from your room when she took her bath. Maybe she took the cleansing milk as well? Check the bathroom."

Bess did. She came out a moment later holding an empty tube. "Looks like she liked it," she said. "She used the whole thing up. And there was more than half a tube in there!"

"Oh, no," I said, wincing. "I should have told her not to go into anyone's room while they weren't there. But I didn't see her until she was coming out. Sorry about that."

Bess smiled wryly. "It's not a big deal," she said. "It's just face wash. Oh, well. I guess Lily just has a thing for other people's stuff—especially mine."

"By the way, how was your evening with her?" George asked me.

"Don't ask," I said gloomily. Lily was starting to give me a headache. I felt sorry for her, and I really wanted to know what had happened to her, but she wasn't making it easy to *like* her.

The sooner I could solve her case and say good-bye to her, the happier I'd be!

In the morning I looked out the window and saw gray skies and fat raindrops rolling down the glass panes. We'd talked about going to see the ruins at Ostia Antica, but the whole complex was outdoors. Given the weather, it seemed that trip would have to wait for another day. *All the better,* I thought. Now I could whisk Lily to the American Embassy, hopefully find out from them who she was, and notify her family and friends that she needed to be taken care of. I might even be rid of her by lunchtime!

The thought gave me a sense of purpose, and I hurried through my shower and breakfast.

Bess, George, and Aunt Estelle had decided to spend the morning seeing the sights in Vatican City. "Are you sure you won't join us?" Aunt Estelle asked me and Lily as we drank our breakfast cappuccino. "The mosaics in the basilica are breathtaking, and of course you shouldn't miss Michelangelo's Pietà."

Lily looked interested. "No, thanks," I said quickly, before she could get a word in. "I wish we could, but we've got to get Lily straightened out. I'm sure there's someone out there who's very worried about her."

"Don't forget, we're meeting Frank and Joe for lunch at I Tre Merli," Bess said.

"I won't," I promised. "I'll meet up with you guys there, okay?"

I carried Lily's and my cups to the sink, and then we headed out. We were lucky enough to get a cab right away in spite of the rain, and I spent the whole ride coaching Lily on walking past the guards at the embassy gates. "They won't hurt you," I promised her. "They may look scary to you, but they're not the bad guys. The feeling you got yesterday when you saw them was very powerful, I know, but it wasn't rational. They're there to protect the embassy, that's all. You need to keep telling yourself that."

"I know you're right," Lily said. "I'll try to control myself."

A few minutes later we pulled up across the street. I

paid the driver and we got out. Lily was pale, but when I gave her a questioning look she nodded. "I'm all right."

"Good girl!" I said approvingly. We crossed the street and walked past the guards without incident. Yes!

Inside we had to go through a metal detector manned by another guard. I could see that Lily was breathing faster, but she got through it all. So far, so good.

We spoke to a receptionist and were directed to the consular section. A plump, balding man with round glasses ushered us into his office, where I explained Lily's problem.

"I'm hoping that she might be in one of your missing persons reports, and we can figure out from that who she is and where she belongs," I concluded.

The consular agent, who'd introduced himself as Bill Lutz, adjusted his glasses. "Amnesia! Goodness, this is one of the most unusual cases I've come across," he said. "Let me have a look."

He turned to his computer and typed a few commands. About twenty head shots popped up, and he turned the screen so that Lily and I could see as he scrolled through them.

"I don't see anyone who looks like you, Lily," I said. Addressing Mr. Lutz, I added, "Is this all there is?"

"That's all we have in our regular missing persons

files at present," he confirmed. "However, we also have a number of files on American children who've allegedly been abducted by one or the other of their parents. You know, in custody cases. Let's have a look through those. She's a bit old for a custody abduction, but you never know."

He typed a few more commands and more head shots popped up on the screen. We scanned them all, but once again there was no one there who looked like Lily. Most of the kids pictured were under ten.

I was starting to feel discouraged. "Is there anyplace else you can think of that we might look?" I appealed to Mr. Lutz.

"I'm afraid not," he said, shaking his head. "I suggest that we take a photo of the young lady right now and get it out to law enforcement agencies in the US. I'll arrange that right now." He picked up the phone and spoke into it briefly. Then, hanging up, he went on. "I'll be frank, though. I'm not sure how effective this will be. The FBI and the police have thousands of missing-person cases, and the chances of the right person seeing the photo are quite small."

Lily's eyes were welling with tears. "No one is looking for me," she whispered.

I felt a spurt of pity. I patted her arm. "Don't worry, we're not giving up," I told her. "There's still the Canadian Consulate to try."

"Good luck," Mr. Lutz told us as we got up to leave.

We stopped off in the passport section and got Lily's picture taken, then headed out. It had stopped raining, and according to my map the Canadian Consulate was relatively near by, so we decided to walk.

After a few blocks the neighborhood changed, becoming more residential and decidedly less luxurious. We were walking down a narrow street lined with nondescript houses when Lily stopped suddenly.

"What's wrong?" I asked, getting ready to run after her if something had freaked her out.

But she had a frown of concentration on her face. "This place is familiar," she said slowly. "I recognize it. I've been here before."

My pulse sped up. "Lily, that's great! Maybe your memory is starting to come back for real!"

Lily walked to the end of the block, then turned and gazed down an even narrower street to her left. "I feel like I should go this way," she said.

It was the opposite direction from the consulate, but I wasn't worried about that. "Fine. Let's go wherever your instinct leads you," I said. "It could well be that we'll learn something about you."

Lily led the way, peering from house to house as we walked slowly down the little street. A thin, middle-aged woman with iron-gray hair and a shapeless black dress was sweeping a stoop with short, vigorous strokes. She paused as we came level with her, her eyes narrowing as she watched us.

Suddenly she darted down the steps and seized Lily by the arm.

"Voi!" she shrieked, clutching Lily's arm and shaking it violently. *"Voi! Io ora ti ho!"*

My Italian was just good enough that after a moment of confusion I thought I understood what she was saying: "You! You! I've got you now!"

CHAPTER **10**

FRANK

TAG-TEAM TACTICS

I crumpled up the paper bag that had held our breakfast rolls. Then, taking careful aim, I lobbed it at my sleeping brother.

It was a direct hit, right in the middle of his forehead. "Glllbbuuuggghhh?" Joe mumbled. He sat up in bed, eyes wild, hair sticking straight up.

"Rise and shine," I told him. "I got you breakfast."

Joe glared at me. "Do you know that you suck?" he said bitterly.

"What can I say, it's just who I am," I told him. "Come on, get up—it's after eight o'clock. I've been up for an hour. I already went out and got rolls and coffee and checked the e-mail." I indicated the laptop, which was open in front of me on the desk.

"Yeah, yeah, aren't you special," Joe grumbled, but he climbed out of bed. Pulling a pair of jeans on over his boxers, he opened the door of our dorm room and disappeared in the direction of the bathroom.

When he reappeared a few moments later, his hair was wet and he looked more human. "After eight—we should get going to the dig," he said. "Even if we're handing in our resignations, it's good to get there on time."

I shook my head. "It's raining. I don't think there'll be any dig work today."

Joe stopped short and gave me a pained look. "So if we don't have to be anywhere special . . . why exactly did you make me get up?"

"Just because we don't have to work at the dig doesn't mean there isn't plenty of other work to do," I said. "Remember the mission?"

"The mission . . . the mission . . . that rings a bell. Oh, right, the mission." Joe sat down at his desk where I'd set our coffees and rolls, and picked up my chocolate croissant (or whatever they call croissants in Italy). He stuffed half of it into his mouth in one bite. "Frank, we solved the case yesterday, remember?" he mumbled through a full mouth. "We're basically done. What's the rush?"

I snatched the croissant out of his hand. "That's mine. And we're not done. You of all people should know that we never say 'mission accomplished' until all the loose ends are tied. How many times have we had cases completely fall apart on us when we thought they were over?"

"Not going to happen this time. You're just mad because I'm the one who cracked it," Joe grumbled.

Ignoring that one, I went to my computer and clicked the mouse. An ATAC dossier opened up on the screen. "Here's the file ATAC put together on Caitlin Boggs—what there is of it," I said.

Joe moved over to stand behind me, peering over my shoulder at the screen. At the top left corner was a small, grainy passport-style photo. It showed a young girl with a heart-shaped face. She looked as if she might be pretty, but like so many passport photos this one was basically a mug shot—her eyes blank, her face set in a weird expression, halfway between a smile and a sneer. Her hair was pulled back into a tight ponytail. The photo was of such poor quality that you couldn't make out her hair or eye color.

"This was taken three years ago, when she was six-teen," I said, reading from the file. "Who knows if she looks anything like this now? Girls can change a lot from sixteen to nineteen. It says her eyes are brown and her hair is auburn."

"Okay, that's no help at all," Joe said. "What else did ATAC dig up?"

"Very little," I said, shaking my head. "She grew up in Grosse Pointe, Michigan. Parents got divorced when she was eight. She lived with her mom—only child. It seems like they had money troubles. Grosse Pointe is a wealthy area, and Caitlin went to a couple of exclusive boarding schools, but Mom declared bankruptcy three times. Dad's a banker, so he has lots of money, but apparently he's never been so good at remembering to pay child support. And Mom likes to live large. According to this report, she spends at least four months of every year at various European spas and ski resorts."

"Ouch," Joe said. "So Caitlin is a poor little rich girl, huh?"

"Sounds that way. She has a juvenile record, too, but it's been sealed by the court and ATAC hasn't been able to get it unsealed yet, so we don't know what she did."

"Let me take three guesses," Joe said. "Shoplifting, or some form of petty theft. Oh, wait, that was only one guess. Classic behavior for a kid who's acting out because her parents ignore her."

I nodded. "It also fits in with what everyone's been saying about her being a shifty character, doesn't it? And it fits with our case, too."

"So here's the recap." Joe walked around the room, ticking points off on his fingers. "Sam Lewis arrives to work on the dig, accompanied by his girlfriend, Caitlin

Boggs. Sam gets Caitlin a job off the books doing office work at BS and T. Caitlin—and this is where we're guessing—steals some artifacts from BS and T for Sam to sell. Sam disappears for a few days, presumably with Caitlin. Then Sam turns up again when he's caught trying to sell said artifacts online. Caitlin is still missing."

"And Sam is scared of something," I added.

"So the big questions are, where is Caitlin now, and what is Sam scared of?" Joe finished.

"Kind of makes you wonder what they were doing during the time they disappeared," I said.

"That is the million-dollar question, isn't it?" Joe agreed.

We looked at each other. "Well, one thing's obvious," I said. "Whatever the answers are, the place to start looking for them is at BS and T."

"Let's stop by the dig first," Joe suggested. "Vanessa will probably be in the office; she said something about needing to catch up on paperwork. I bet I can ask her to come up with some legitimate excuse for us to go down to BS and T. That way we have a cover story if we need one."

"Good plan," I agreed.

We hopped on the Metro and took it to the Colosseum stop. From there we headed up and around the Palatine Hill, going through the staff entrance. Walking around the huge ruins in the rain was eerie—without the hordes of tourists there, it was silent and other-worldly. Shreds of fog drifted between the downed columns like lost ghosts.

As it turned out, even though no one was working on the quadrants, there was plenty of activity at the dig site. I spotted Jeff and Kyra going into the trailer where the artifacts were cataloged. As the door opened, I caught sight of a tall, stooped figure already inside—Claude Bonaire. Apparently they were all spending the rainy day studying the latest finds.

Vanessa was in her office, as Joe had predicted. He explained to her what we needed and she nodded. "That's easy," she said. "I actually need some more shipping crates sent up from BS and T anyway. You can go down there and get them for me. I'll call Joanna and let her know you're coming."

"Just Joe," I said quickly. "I'd appreciate it if you didn't mention me."

Vanessa looked intrigued, but didn't say anything as she pulled out her phone and quickly set up the crate pickup.

"Is there any news on my . . . my problem?" she asked in a hesitant voice as she closed her phone.

"We contacted some of our colleagues who work in the organized crime task force in London," I told her. "They've been watching Fat Hamish for another case, so they know all about him already."

"Apparently they're planning some kind of major sting operation, and it's likely that in a couple of days Fat Hamish will have much more pressing things to worry about than collecting debts from your brother," Joe added. "We'll keep you posted, but I think your brother should be in the clear soon."

Vanessa put her hand on her chest. "Oh, that is such a relief to hear!" she said, closing her eyes for a moment. "So Tony'll be safe? And I won't have to keep making the fake pots? You boys are lifesavers! Anything you need from me, anything at all, you've only got to ask."

"Good to know. Thanks!" I said. Then Joe and I headed toward the train station.

We reviewed our strategy as we walked from the terminal in Civitavecchia to the BS&T warehouse. "All you have to do is get Joanna into the warehouse and keep her there for a few minutes," I told Joe. "Oh, and let's sync our phones so I can listen in on your conversation. That way I'll know if you're coming back toward the offices."

Our phones, in addition to all their other excellent features, had a function that allowed one of them to work as a mike and the other as a receiver, so that conversations one of us was having could be heard by the other person, even at a distance. The range wasn't huge—the listening phone couldn't pick up a signal from more than five hundred yards away—but it should work for what we were doing today.

We stopped and quickly set up the phones. It meant Joe had to wear a hands-free device, like people use when they drive, but that was common enough these days that it wouldn't seem suspicious.

"So have you come up with some conversation topics to keep her busy?" I asked as the offices came in sight.

Joe snorted. "I don't need topics, Frank. I know how to talk to girls. If all else fails, I can just tell her how pretty she is."

"I don't think that would work on Joanna," I warned. "She doesn't strike me as the type who falls for pickup lines."

"How would you know?" Joe said with a grin. "Did you try one on her?"

I whacked him on the side of his head. "Shut up. Listen, I noticed a flag hanging over her desk that I didn't recognize, so I looked it up on line last night. It's Corsican. I suspect she's Corsican too—she was wearing a pin with the same symbol that was on the flag. If you run out of things to talk to her about, you could ask her about that."

"Corsica? Is that somewhere in Greece?" Joe asked.

I shook my head sadly. "Your ignorance is monumental, you know that? No, it's not in Greece, dummy.

It's an island off the Italian coast, pretty close to Rome. Maybe two hundred miles away. It's where Napoléon Bonaparte was born."

"Napoléon?" Joe repeated. "But wasn't he French?"

"Well, Corsica is controlled by France, even though most of the people who live there are of Italian descent. In fact, I read last night that there's a pretty serious movement for Corsican independence. Some of the pro-independence groups have even threatened violence."

"Fascinating," Joe said, pretending to yawn. "I'm sure she'll be riveted when I start talking about Corsican independence."

"You never know," I pointed out. "Just trying to give you some extra ammunition, little brother."

"You worry too much. I'll be fine," Joe assured me. "Okay, you stay out of sight. I'm going in."

I watched him walk toward the office building. Right before he went inside he spoke into his mike. "Can you hear me?"

He turned around and I gave him a thumbs-up from where I stood. He nodded and went in.

I listened while he explained who he was. Thanks to Vanessa's phone call, Joanna had been expecting him, so he had no trouble in getting her to take him out to the warehouse. As soon as they disappeared into the shadowy interior, I hurried through the door and over to the filing cabinets by the far wall.

I knew I had to work fast, and I did, yanking open the file drawers and scanning for personnel files. As my eyes skimmed over file labels, I listened to Joe trying to make conversation with Joanna. It went something like this:

Joe: "So what's a beautiful girl like you doing hidden away in a dingy place like this?"

Joanna: No reply.

Joe (clearing throat): "So—the shipping business, huh? Is that interesting?"

Joanna: "It's my job."

Joe: "Ha-ha, that's honest. Hey, what about Rome? What a great city. Great nightlife. I bet you go out to a different club every night of the week."

Joanna: No reply.

My brother was striking out. Even though I knew it meant I'd have even less time to snoop, I couldn't help grinning to myself. I'd warned him she was tough! I closed the drawer I'd been looking in, which seemed to be all cargo manifests for the Civitavecchia fleet, and opened the next one. Hmmm, more of same.

Joe: "Those are some big dogs you've got there. Do you really need guard dogs for a place like this? It seems pretty quiet."

Joanna: "It's best to be prepared for anything."

Joe: "Prepared for what? Have you ever had any incidents?"

Joanna: "The crates are right over here."

Uh-oh. He was really striking out big time. They were already almost done with their business in the warehouse! I quickly opened a third drawer. Yes! *Personale*, read the label on the front hanging file. I was reasonably sure that meant "personnel." Now, if I could just find some reference to Caitlin Boggs in here . . .

Joe (starting to sound tense): "So . . . do you live in Rome?"

Joanna: "No."

Joe: "Oh, really? Where do you live?"

Joanna: "Are you going to take the crates or not?"

Man, she was all business! I needed more time, not least because all the labels and files were in Italian. I quickly texted Joe: keep her there! need more time!

Joe (sounding increasingly desperate): "So I noticed there's a Corsican flag hanging over your desk. Are you Corsican?"

Joanna (surprised): "You know the Corsican flag?"

Joe (laughs): "Doesn't everybody?"

Joanna: "Not everyone, no. I would not say that."

Joe: "Well, it's very recognizable. You know, I've always thought that Corsica should be independent from France. It doesn't make any sense, especially since most Corsicans aren't even French by descent!"

Joanna: "I completely agree. We are Italian, in our language, our culture, our roots. But, you know, most people don't even realize Corsica is struggling for independence. I'm impressed by how much you know."

Joe (modestly): "I guess I just like to be informed."

Oh, he was good. I had to give him that. My little brother was a world-class con artist. You'd never guess that I'd just fed him that information ten minutes ago. . . .

They were chatting away now, Joe feeding her questions and Joanna talking about the independence movement. Although her voice stayed calm, it was clear to me that a free Corsica was near and dear to her heart.

I closed the personnel drawer. As far as I could tell, there was no file on Caitlin Boggs. Not surprising, since she'd apparently been employed unofficially, but still, it was disappointing. Where could she have vanished to?

Maybe there'd be some sign of her on Joanna's desk. I hurried over and started sifting through papers.

Near the bottom of a stack of messages I found a pink phone message slip addressed to Joanna. It was dated from the previous week, and it said "Mr. Mazzini called. Wants you to come out to island to inspect progress of project." It was signed "Caitlin."

Yes! There it was—a sign that she'd been here, that she was real and not a phantom. I wondered if Joe could come up with a way to ask about her without making Joanna suspicious.

As I glanced around the room, seeking inspiration, my eye landed on a smallish photo that hung on the wall next to the Corsican flag. It showed a tall, craggy-faced man smashing a bottle over the prow of a ship—a launching ceremony, I guessed.

And the man in the photo was Claude Bonaire, the millionaire from our dig.

I did a double take. What in the world . . . ? It was so unexpected. What was a photo of Claude Bonaire doing in the offices of BS&T?

Wait. Wasn't Bonaire a shipping magnate—hadn't Jeff told me that?

I ran back to the file cabinet and opened the drawer of shipping manifests again. I yanked one of the manifests out of its file. The BS&T company logo, a large *B* with a smaller *S&T* stacked to its right, was prominent at the bottom of the page. And now that I was paying attention, I saw what I hadn't noticed before. Underneath the *S&T*, which presumably stood for "Shipping and Transit," small letters spelled out the name that the *B* stood for. It was Bonaire.

So BS&T was Bonaire Shipping and Transit. Claude Bonaire owned the company that shipped artifacts from the dig, the company for which Caitlin Boggs had worked and from which she and Sam had stolen the artifacts Sam tried to sell.

My head was spinning. This was a new twist indeed.

Was Bonaire involved somehow in the stolen artifacts? Or with Caitlin's disappearance? Jeff had said that Bonaire spent a lot of time talking to Sam. Were they involved in some scheme together, or was it just a coincidence?

I thought of Joe that morning, saying the case was closed, and me arguing with him. Usually I like winning arguments with my little brother.

But this time I just had a sinking feeling that things were about to get a lot more complicated.

CHAPTER 11

NANCY

EXAMINING A LIFE

"Io ora ti ho!" the old woman shouted again, shaking Lily's arm.

"Let me go! Help!" Lily shrieked. She scrabbled ineffectively at the woman's fingers. "Don't let her hurt me—make her let me go! Somebody help me!"

I stood there with my mouth open in shock, watching the bizarre struggle. The elderly woman was, if anything, smaller and lighter than Lily, who was maybe five foot two and slender. I felt like I should put a hand on each of their heads and hold them apart from each other while they tired themselves out.

Instead I gently but firmly pried the elderly woman's fingers off Lily's arm. Then I pushed Lily behind me as I spoke to the woman. *"Mi despiace,"* I said. *"Non parlamos buon Italiano. Voi parla Inglese?"*

"I speak little English," the woman said, still panting and shooting angry glances at Lily over my shoulder.

"I'm not sure why you are angry," I said. "My friend here has lost her memory. She cannot remember anything. Do you know her?"

"Si, I know her. *Si, si, la ragazza, io la so, lei è cattiva . . ."* And the woman started rattling on in rapid Italian. I held up my hands pleadingly.

"Please, in English," I said. "I'm sorry."

The woman made an effort to pull herself together. "I know her," she said. "She rent room from me. And she no pay me! 'Oh, Signora Alberti, I have it tomorrow, tomorrow, tomorrow,'"—the woman mimicked Lily's breathy voice—"but never she have money, never. Three week she owe to me, and then, *pffft!* She disappear!"

"I have *amnesia!*" Lily shrilled, as if the woman should somehow know this already. "It wasn't my fault!"

I was trying to process all this. We'd found Lily's landlord! What a lucky chance! Now we'd certainly be able to find out more about Lily herself!

"Signora Alberti, we're very sorry," I said. "Something happened to Lily. We're not sure what. But she has lost her memory. That's why she disappeared.

She never meant to leave without paying the rent." I said this as sincerely as I could, though from what I'd seen of Lily, I was by no means certain it was true.

"Yeah!" Lily agreed. She folded her arms and sniffed.

"Hmmph," Signora Alberti muttered, glaring at Lily with deep suspicion.

"Did she by any chance sign a rental agreement?" I asked. A document like that would have her name, and probably other information like her parents' or guardians' names or a home address in the States.

"I don't ask for piece of paper!" Signora Alberti's expression darkened. "I am honest woman. I think others are honest too. I say, 'You live here, you pay me one hundred euros every week, I give you nice room, wash your clothes.' That is all." Bright red patches were starting to appear on her cheeks. "But she no pay!"

"I'd be happy to pay what Lily owes you," I said quickly. I hoped it wouldn't be too much, but Signora Alberti was right, she deserved to be paid—and if she had the money, she'd be more likely to want to help us. I had a couple of traveler's checks with me that I could use to pay her if need be.

"*Es cento euro*—one hundred euros every week," Signora Alberti announced. "She owe for three weeks and five days. I take *trecento cinquanta*—three hundred and fifty."

I gulped. Three hundred and fifty euros was more

than I had. But maybe she'd accept a down payment. "I can give you two hundred right now, and I promise to bring you the rest later today," I said, crossing my fingers that she'd say yes. "Signora, Lily and I really need to get into her room. We may be able to find something there that tells us who she is."

"Hmmmmm." Signora Alberti pursed her lips. *"Non so . . . non so . . ."*

I took a deep breath. I really didn't want to do this, but it was an emergency. "I can also give you my credit card to hold," I added. "That way you'll know I have to come back."

Signora Alberti looked me over. Then she nodded once. "No credit card," she said. *"You* I think I trust." Her withering glance at Lily said clearly enough what she didn't say in words.

"Thank you very much." I signed over the traveler's checks to her. Then she led me and Lily through a small, dark foyer, out into a tiny but sunny courtyard, and to a room by itself at the far side. She unlocked the door with a key she took from the pocket of her shapeless black dress. "I wait here," she said.

Lily's room was not luxurious, but it was clean and pleasant. At least, there were no dust bunnies or cobwebs. But clearly Lily wasn't much of a housekeeper. Crumpled clothes were strewn over the single bed, the table and chairs, and the terra-cotta tiled floor. American fashion magazines were tossed carelessly here and there. An MP3 player and a framed photo sat on a small nightstand.

Lily crossed to the photo and picked it up. I heard the sharp intake of her breath as she stared at it.

"That's Sam," she said. "Sam and me."

She was remembering! I hurried to her and peered over her shoulder. The photo was of Lily and a tall guy with shaggy dirty blond or light brown hair and a lopsided smile. His face was tilted down, Lily's tilted up, so that they were gazing into each other's eyes. Lily looked radiant.

They were arm in arm on what appeared to be a snowy college campus. Behind them I could see brick buildings and crowds of bundled-up student types.

"Sam?" I repeated, trying to keep the urgency out of my voice. "Is he your boyfriend?"

Lily nodded. I could hear from the tremble in her voice that she was trying not to cry. "He loves me. He always takes care of me."

"What's his last name?"

She was silent for a long moment. Then she looked up at me, her eyes brimming. "I can't remember. I can't remember where this picture was taken, or who took it. I just know that's Sam, and we love each other. But I don't know where he is."

After a second the tears fell. She didn't sob. Big drops

just ran silently down her cheeks, as if there was an ocean behind her eyes. Somehow she seemed even more forlorn now than she had when I first found her.

"We'll find him," I promised, putting an arm around her shoulders. "And you know, he's got to be searching for you too. You can tell by the look on his face how much he loves you."

Lily nodded, the tears flowing faster.

I gave her shoulders a gentle squeeze, then left her to collect herself while I prowled around the room.

But there was nothing more to find. No passport tucked away in a drawer, no credit card receipts, no wallet with driver's license or student ID. Nor was there any mail—no postcard or letters addressed to her, no computer with e-mail. The magazines had all been bought at newsstands, so there were no address labels on them.

I bit my lip. This case was getting frustrating! How could a person's life be so hard to track down?

My stomach gave a twinge, reminding me that it had been a while since breakfast. I checked my watch and was startled to see that it was already past noon. We were going to be late for our lunch with Joe and Frank Hardy.

The Hardys! *They might be able to help me*, I thought. First of all, talking things out with them would be useful in itself—they were experienced investigators and might be able to come up with some suggestions for turning up new leads. But even more than that, through them I could perhaps get ATAC to use its manpower and technological power to uncover Lily's real identity.

"We should get going," I said. "We've got a lunch date."

"Maybe I'll just stay here," Lily said in a dreary voice. "I don't really feel like eating."

"Cheer up! We're going to figure this out," I said briskly. "My friends Frank and Joe are detectives too. And we're getting somewhere, we really are. We found where you live, and we found out about Sam, and . . ." Another idea struck me. "And we might be able to figure out from this photo what college you go to."

"I guess." Lily didn't look up.

"In the meantime, you need to eat, and so do I. So come on, let's go get some lunch."

She followed me obediently out of her room and across the courtyard. We said good-bye to Signora Alberti and I promised her we'd be back with the rest of the rent that evening. Then we went out to the street and hailed a taxi.

I gave Lily a discreet sidelong glance as she settled into the back seat of the taxi. She stared mutely out the window. Her face looked wan and sad. I almost wished for the old, jittery Lily. This silent shadow was a bit worrisome.

Unfortunately traffic was awful, and even the skill of our driver, a grizzled man who didn't speak to us but steered in and out of tiny openings with ferocious concentration, couldn't keep us moving. The closer we got to the river, the worse things got. I tried in vain not to fidget as we came to a stop for the third time in less than a block. Masses of tourists and office workers on their lunch break flowed around the car, oblivious to me sitting inside twiddling my thumbs.

After we'd sat in the cab for over twenty minutes, I decided we might be better off walking. We were a few blocks west of our destination, but there appeared to be some sort of demonstration blocking the street ahead of us, and I was afraid that if we stayed in the cab we'd still be sitting there hours later.

I paid the driver and climbed out, Lily in tow. "This way," I said, taking her hand and leading her down the street. We'd have to find a way around the demonstration. Bunches of people wearing white headbands waved signs and shouted on front of a massive brick building with white columns and row upon row of windows.

I looked at the signs. Of course they were in Italian, but some had pictures on them rather than words. The picture that was on most of them was a striking drawing of a black head silhouetted on a white background. The head was wrapped in a white bandanna, much like the headbands the protesters were wearing.

I still had Lily by the hand. Suddenly I felt her grip tighten spasmodically on mine. I glanced at her.

Her eyes were two circles, perfectly round with terror, as she gaped at something over my shoulder. I whirled to see what she was looking at.

One of the protesters, a big, hulking dark-haired man wearing a white bandana and plain green army fatigues, was staring back at us with a shocked look on his face.

I had only a split second to study him before my arm was nearly jerked out of its socket. "Run," Lily said breathlessly in my ear. "Run!"

And then, with a strength I never dreamed she was capable of, she dragged me away through the crowd.

"Who was that man?" I demanded as I stumbled after her. "Why are we running?"

Lily didn't answer, just plowed ahead.

I turned to look over my shoulder, hoping I could get a better look at the guy.

As it turned out, I got a very good look at him—because he was coming after us, moving fast, shoving people out of his way right and left. There was an ugly scowl on his face. Was he someone else Lily had ripped off?

Then I saw his hand come out of his pocket and

beckon to someone off to his right. My breath caught in my throat as I saw the wink of metal. He had a knife!

Whoever this man was, he meant business—and I really didn't want to find out what that business was!

JOE

ANSWERS AT LAST?

"Well, of course, Pascal Paoli, the father of the Corsican nation, was one of the most brilliant men of a brilliant age," Joanna Paoli said.

I perched on the edge of a stack of shipping crates and tried to keep my expression fascinated. "Of course," I agreed.

"I don't know if you know this, but Pascal Paoli wrote the constitution that Corsica adopted in 1755, more than twenty years before the creation of the American constitution," Joanna went on. "It was far ahead of its time. It even gave women the right to vote!"

She'd been lecturing away happily for the last ten minutes without me contributing more than the occasional "hmm" or "yes," but with her gaze on me,

I felt I had to say a bit more. "No, I wasn't aware of that," I said. "Wow! That's—that's—"

"True genius, yes, I know," Joanna finished for me. Her green eyes were sparkling and her cheeks were slightly pink. She was awfully pretty. Maybe a little too obsessed with Corsican history, but I was willing to overlook it as long as I could keep staring at her.

"The Genoese could not control Corsica, so they gave it to the French," Joanna was saying. "The French—pffft! What do they know of the Corsican soul? They claimed to be for liberty, equality, and fraternity, but all they have given us is two centuries of oppression."

My cell phone vibrated and I sneaked a discreet look at the screen. 2 more min, read Frank's latest text.

Not a problem, I thought, hiding a grin. I was doing a stellar job of keeping Joanna occupied. True, it had been touch and go there at the beginning, when she was so frosty to me. And yes, it was also true that the way I'd gotten her to open up had been to use Frank's topic—Corsican independence. Hard to believe that my big brother had actually supplied an icebreaker that worked on a girl. But whatever—Joanna was now responding perfectly to the Joe Hardy charm. I could keep this up all day. I was even starting to wonder if she'd go out on a date with me. I wondered how she felt about younger men. . . .

I thought of my next line. "Paoli," I said, wrinkling my forehead. "That's your last name, too, isn't it? Are you any relation to"—I couldn't remember the guy's first name, so I just used his title—"to, um, the Father of Corsica?"

Joanna's cheeks turned even pinker. "Only a very distant connection," she said, looking down. "But yes, Pascal Paoli is my ancestor."

"Wow. You must be very proud," I said. "It's kind of like—like being related to George Washington."

My phone vibrated again. I glanced at it while Joanna was gazing modestly at her feet. gag me! I read. done here. meet at train station. ask about claude bonaire. he owns bs&t!!!

My eyebrows rose. *That* was interesting!

The shipping crates I'd supposedly come here for, flattened for transport, were stacked on a wheeled dolly. I took the handle and began pushing it toward the front of the warehouse. Joanna walked beside me. "Hey, so the guy who owns your company works on our dig," I said.

Joanna shrugged. "Yes, that's right," she agreed.

"What's he like?" I asked. "He seems a little, well, obsessed with that old Roman king dude, Claudius." Frank had told me about Bonaire's Claudius lecture.

Joanna smiled scornfully. "He's a silly man," she said. "He believes he is the descendant of Claudius. He has even had a genealogist create a family tree showing how he is related. He *worships* Claudius."

Kind of like she worshipped Pascal Paoli, I thought but didn't say.

"His proudest possession is a fragment of a scroll that was believed to be part of Claudius's library." Joanna laughed. "But he is harmless. He stays out of my way."

Hmmm. I wasn't sure what, if anything, Frank wanted me to find out, but I couldn't really think of any more questions about Bonaire. I decided to take a shot at something else, on my own.

"By the way, I had a buddy on the dig," I said. Reaching the loading bay, I parked the dolly and wiped my forehead. "He told me his girlfriend was working for BS and T. Caitlin Boggs. I'm wondering if you've seen her lately—I've been trying to get in touch with her."

Joanna's eyes went blank for a fraction of a second. Then she shook her head. "I don't know who you mean," she said. "There is nobody else working here. Just me and the warehouse men."

If I hadn't seen that brief flash of something in her eyes, I would have believed her. But I had seen it. And I knew Joanna was lying.

Why, though? Surely she wasn't worried about me reporting BS&T for hiring undocumented workers. Not that I was an expert on Italian labor laws, but I couldn't believe it would be that big a deal.

Why else would she lie about Caitlin having worked there?

Unless she had something to do with Caitlin's disappearance. . . .

I didn't see any way to push the questions at the moment without raising her suspicions. But maybe I could arrange another meeting. At, say, a nice restaurant.

"I've really enjoyed talking to you," I began. "How about you and me—"

"Yes, it has been interesting," Joanna interrupted, "but I must get back to work now. Tell Vanessa that if she needs more crates I will send one of my men to the dig."

"Well, I'll bring the dolly back later to—"

"There is no need. We have hundreds of them. Good-bye."

I winced. It was a brush-off, no question about it.

She was holding out her hand to shake. I took it, and with a brief, cool nod, she went striding back toward her office.

Thoughtfully I headed for the train station. The drizzle had eased off now, but the air was unpleasantly damp and clammy.

Frank was waiting for me on one of the benches.

"Did you catch that last bit?" I asked, throwing myself down beside him.

"You mean the part where Joanna blew you off?" Frank asked, smirking. "I heard it."

I jabbed him with my elbow. "She blew me off all right, but not because she didn't like me. The old Joe Hardy charm was working just fine, until I mentioned Caitlin. That's when she shut down."

"Shut *you* down, you mean," Frank said, but he was frowning.

"I'm positive she was lying," I told him as we climbed aboard the train.

"Which makes you wonder why." We chose our seats and Frank helped me stow the crates on the overhead rack. Then he resumed, "If Caitlin stopped showing up for work because she and Sam went off on some crazy trip, like we've been assuming, Joanna wouldn't need to hide that from anyone. But if Caitlin *didn't* disappear of her own free will . . ."

"Exactly," I said with a nod.

Frank ran his fingers through his short dark hair in frustration. "I don't know where this is all going," he said. "We came here to investigate a possible theft ring. So far we've got nothing on the theft ring, but we do have a missing girl and a suspicious shipping company run by a beautiful Corsican nationalist."

"And owned by an American nutball who thinks he's the emperor Claudius's great-great-great-grandson," I reminded him. "Let's not forget the nutball."

Frank smiled wryly. "No, let's not," he said. Pulling out his phone, he opened an Internet connection and typed a rapid e-mail. "I'm asking ATAC for anything they can give us on Claude Bonaire and BS and T," he told me. "Although I don't see how or why there could be a connection there. If this case does have anything to do with a theft ring—though I'm starting to be fairly sure it doesn't—then Bonaire being involved doesn't make any sense. Sure, he's a nut for anything to do with Emperor Claudius, but my guess is, he's got enough money that he could *buy* the Emerald Bower lock, stock, and barrel if he wanted."

He put away his phone and cracked his knuckles. "Looks like the weather is clearing," he said, looking out the train window.

"Just in time for our lunch with three cute girls. We're meeting Nancy, George, and Bess at that restaurant at one," I reminded him.

"I remember." Frank's face lit up. "You know, I'd really like to hear what Nancy thinks about this mess. I know it's against the rules to talk about our missions to non-ATAC people, but she's different, isn't she?"

I turned away to hide my smile. Frank was starting to loosen up!

We got back to the city and dropped the crates at the dig site. Claude Bonaire was still in the cataloging and classification trailer, but there were a lot of other people in there too, so it didn't seem like the right time to try to question him. Besides, if we didn't move it we'd be late for lunch.

When we arrived at the restaurant, though, we found Bess and George, but no Nancy. "She's meeting us here," George explained. She grinned. "She had a little mystery that she needed to solve before lunch."

My eyebrows rose. "Say what?"

"See, the thing you have to realize about Nancy Drew is, mysteries seek her out," Bess said. "Yesterday a girl picked my pocket near the Trevi Fountain. Nancy and George caught her, and it turned out she's an American with amnesia."

"Which doesn't prevent her from being a royal pain," George put in.

"So true," Bess agreed, rolling her eyes. I grinned. The two of them were almost like a comedy act.

"Amnesia, huh?" I said as we followed our waiter to a table. "Tell us more."

So, over antipasto, Bess and George shared the strange and fascinating story of Lily, the forgetful thief. "Anyway, Nancy took her to the American Embassy this morning to try to find out who she is and get her taken care of," Bess concluded. She glanced at her watch. "She's almost twenty minutes late. I hope she didn't run into any trouble."

"There she is now," Frank said, half-rising from his chair to wave Nancy over to us. "She's got a girl with her. Is that Lily?"

"It is," George confirmed, sounding irked. "I guess Nancy didn't manage to get in touch with her family yet."

As Nancy and the strange girl threaded their way through the tables toward us, I saw that Nancy's cheeks were pink and her eyes bright, as if she'd been running. The girl just looked terrified, all huge eyes in a heart-shaped face.

She also looked familiar. I tilted my head as I stared at her, trying to figure out where I'd seen her before. Out of the corner of my eye I saw Frank doing the same thing.

"Sorry we're late," Nancy said as she slid into an empty seat. "Frank, Joe, this is Lily. Well, that's what we're calling her because we don't know her real name yet. I'm guessing Bess and George have filled you in?"

"We just finished," Bess said, biting into a piece of bread dipped in olive oil. "What happened to you guys? Lily, you look like you've seen a ghost."

"Not a ghost," Nancy said grimly. "But we did see a very large man with a knife, who happened to be chasing us."

"What?" we all said at once.

"It wasn't too far from here. There were a bunch of protesters demonstrating outside some building. One of them caught sight of Lily and I'm pretty sure he recognized her, though I have no idea where from," Nancy told us. "And he came after us. With a knife. We managed to lose him in the crowd, but it was scary." She turned to Lily. "Are you sure you don't know who he was?"

Lily shook her head. "I told you, the minute I saw him I knew I should be scared of him—but I don't know why," she said, her voice trembling. She stood up. "I—I need to go splash cold water on my face. I'll be right back." Without waiting for a reply, she headed for the restrooms.

"Hey, Nan, it sounds like Lily reacted to this guy the same way she reacted to the security guards at the embassy yesterday," George pointed out.

"Right," Nancy agreed. She snapped her fingers. "You know, this guy was wearing army fatigues too. Like the guards."

"What else did you notice about him?" Frank asked, leaning forward. "Were they American Army fatigues? Italian? From somewhere else?"

Nancy bit her lip. "I'm not sure," she admitted. "They were plain green, that's all I know. Not camo. Oh, and he was wearing a white headband. Lots of the protesters were wearing those. I think it had to do with their flag, which was white with a black silhouette of a head in the middle, wearing a white headband."

I think my eyes practically bugged out of my head. Nancy had just described the Corsican flag! Talk about bizarre coincidences!

"No way!" I blurted out.

"You're not serious!" Frank said at the same moment.

Nancy looked at us with raised eyebrows. "I'm totally serious," she said. "Why? Does that flag mean something to you?"

"It's the Corsican flag," Frank said. "We know that because it's come up in the case we're working on."

Nancy's blue eyes widened. "Go on."

So Frank and I told them all about our investigation, and BS&T, and Joanna Paoli. "Joanna knows something about our missing girl, Caitlin," I said. "*And* she's a rabid Corsican nationalist, like the protesters you just saw."

"And I'm wondering if that's a coincidence," Frank added.

Nancy nodded. "I'm right with you," she said.

"I'm not sure *I* am," Bess said plaintively, but no one paid any attention. Frank, Nancy, and I all had the same feeling—that we were right on the edge of a huge discovery.

"Remind me—what was the name of the guy who

was arrested for trying to sell the artifacts?" Nancy asked urgently.

"Sam Lewis," Frank supplied.

Reaching into her raincoat pocket, Nancy drew out a small framed photograph and handed it across the table to us. "Is that him, by any chance?"

Frank and I put our heads together to study the snapshot. Sam Lewis grinned out of it, his arm around a beaming Lily.

And now I realized why Lily looked so familiar. I'd seen her passport photo, but it was three years out of date.

"That's him. More to the point, that's *her*," Frank said, his voice soft with amazement. "That's Caitlin Boggs. Nancy, your amnesia victim is our missing girl!"

13

NANCY

KICKED OUT!

"Oh, this is too weird" was all I could say.

My case and the Hardys' had just turned out to be one and the same! What were the odds on something like that?

"Don't look now, but here comes Lily—I mean, Caitlin," Bess said.

The girl we'd been calling Lily sat down at our table and gave us all a watery smile. Her face looked freshly scrubbed. "Did I miss something?" she asked.

Frank's neck turned red and Joe coughed. I cleared my throat.

"As a matter of fact, you did. You're not going to believe this," I said, "but my friends Frank and Joe here have been working on a case of their own—and it turns out you're part of it. We know your real identity now."

Her brown eyes went round with shock. "Are you serious? Tell me! Tell me!"

"Your name is Caitlin Boggs," Frank said, taking over with a glance at me.

"Caitlin," she repeated. "Caitlin . . ." She nodded slowly. "Yes, that's right. That *is* my name."

"You came here with your boyfriend, whose name is Sam Lewis. He's a student of archaeology," Frank added.

"Sam." Caitlin's face softened. "I remember that part now! I remember!"

"Great!" George said. "Now, do you remember—"

I waved her to silence. I didn't want to push Caitlin too hard yet.

"Where is Sam?" Caitlin asked urgently. "Is he all right?"

"Not exactly," Joe said. "He's not hurt, but he's been arrested for trying to sell stolen artifacts online."

Caitlin's face paled. "But that doesn't . . ." She trailed off.

"Do you remember that bit?" I asked her, watching her closely.

She avoided my eyes. "I . . . I . . ."

"Go on," George drawled.

"I don't exactly remember," Caitlin said.

I waited.

"I really don't," she said, raising her eyes to mine. "Everything from the time we got to Rome is hazy, and I can't remember anything at all from the last couple of weeks." She swallowed hard. "But I do remember that I tried to talk Sam into taking a few of the artifacts from the dig. I figured between us we could fix it so no one would notice they were gone, and it seemed like an easy way to make some real money."

"You *tried* to talk Sam into it?" Joe repeated. "You mean he wouldn't do it?"

Caitlin smiled wryly. "Not my Sam," she replied. "He practically had a heart attack when I suggested it. He's totally straight. It's part of what makes him so lovable."

Frank leaned back in his seat and pressed the tips of his fingers together. "Hmm. Well, he definitely did steal artifacts, there's no doubt about that. So the question is, if he's that much of a straight arrow, what made him do it?"

"That's what I want to know," Caitlin said softly. "Because it doesn't make any sense."

"Unless he had a very good reason," I said, thinking out loud. "Like maybe someone was threatening him. Or you. And he really, really needed the money."

Frank and Joe looked at each other and nodded. "That could fit in with what we saw on Sam's interrogation tape," Joe told us. "It seemed clear that he was scared of something or someone. That's why he wasn't talking."

"It would really help us—and maybe it would help Sam too—if you could try to remember something about what happened to you the past week," Frank told Caitlin. His voice was gentle, nonthreatening. "Just let your mind wander. See if anything comes to you."

"Maybe something connected with men in uniforms," I added. Caitlin's reaction to the men in fatigues had been so strong.

Caitlin's face twisted with anxiety. "I want to remember. I really do. But when I try to think about it, it's like there's a big mirror wall in my mind. It's like something is stopping me from focusing on it. Do you know what I mean?"

I nodded. "I do know what you mean," I assured her, putting my hand on her arm. "I believe that something really scary happened to you and Sam, and your mind isn't letting you remember because you aren't ready to deal with it. But the trouble is, we really need to deal with it."

"I know," Caitlin said miserably.

"Maybe it can wait until after lunch, though," Bess suggested. "I for one am starving, and we haven't even ordered yet."

"I'm with Bess. I always think better on a full stomach," Joe said.

"Not that that's saying much," Frank cracked.

We all laughed, and that broke the somber mood.

Over a family-style lunch of salad and an incredible pasta dish with tomatoes and olives, Caitlin told us a little about herself. As she spoke, it became sadly obvious why no one had raised an alarm about her going missing.

"My mom's been staying at Canyon Lake Spa for the last month," she said with a grimace. "She calls it a 'meditation retreat.' I call it rehab. But whatever. She told me she'd be unreachable during that time. And my dad . . ." She shrugged. "I haven't talked to him in two years. I'm sure he has no idea I even went to Rome in the first place." Tossing her head, she added, "And if he did, he wouldn't care."

"Oh, that can't be true," Bess protested.

"Believe me, it is," Caitlin said.

"Well, even so, we should get in touch with one or both of them," I said. "They're your family, and they need to know what's happened to you."

"They're not my family. Sam is my family," Caitlin said simply. "Can't I see him?"

Frank laid his fork down and wiped his mouth. "Joe and I will try to set that up, but it'll probably take a day at least. We're dealing with government bureaucracy here, and nothing ever moves quickly in a bureaucracy."

"The Italian authorities will probably need to talk to you anyway," Joe added. "They'll want to see if you can fill in any of the holes in Sam's story."

"But I can't," Caitlin said, looking panicky. "I have no idea why Sam stole those things. Do I really have to talk to them?"

I spoke up quickly, wanting to keep her from melting down. "The nice thing is, at least we know where you live now," I pointed out. "You can stay in your own place tonight. Won't that feel good?"

To my dismay, Caitlin looked even more panicked. She began shaking her head violently. "No!" she blurted out. "You want me to stay in that place? After that man nearly caught us today? What if he's still after me? Nancy, I can't! I'm terrified!"

She looked down and began twisting her cloth napkin in her hands. Over her bent head, I exchanged glances with Bess and George. I could tell they were feeling the same way I was. On the one hand, none of us really wanted Caitlin to stay with us for another night of our vacation. On the other hand, how could we possibly abandon her? She so badly needed friends who would stick by her and help her. And it was only one more night. By tomorrow, we'd have contacted her parents and Sam, and in all likelihood she'd be on her way home.

"Don't worry, you can come back with us. I'm sure

Aunt Estelle won't mind," George said after a moment.

Caitlin peeked up at us. "Thanks," she said in a small voice.

We finished lunch and went to a gelato place for dessert. Afterward the Hardy brothers walked us to the Metro. Frank and I were a few paces behind the others. "So, have you managed to have any fun in Rome yet, or has it been all business?" I asked him.

"Oh, well, we've . . . uh . . . we've been working pretty hard on the case," he said with a self-conscious smile. I couldn't help being amused. He was such a smart, together guy, but he was so flustered by talking to a girl! I couldn't resist teasing him a little.

"No nightlife for you?" I asked. "No going out dancing? No asking a pretty girl out on a date? Rome is supposed to be the city for love, you know. And I bet there are tons of girls here who would just swoon over you."

Poor Frank's face was the color of a tomato. "Uh— well—I'm not really—," he stammered.

I burst out laughing. "Oh, Frank, I'm just teasing!"

He laughed too, a little stiffly. "I knew that."

"Sorry." I tucked my hand under his elbow. "I didn't mean to embarrass you."

He looked sheepish. "I embarrass easily. It's okay."

We walked in silence for a moment, me still holding his arm. I saw that his face was still red, but he was smiling a real smile now.

At the Metro stop we said our good-byes. I took Frank's number and promised to call him later that afternoon so he could tell us the update from ATAC.

"Well, this case seems to be wrapping up more neatly than usual," George commented as we boarded the train.

"I know," I agreed. "I'd still really like to find out what happened to Caitlin during the time she was missing, but I'm not sure where to go from here." I shrugged, trying to shed the feeling of unfinished business. "I guess the important thing is that we've found out who she really is, and she'll be taken care of."

Twenty minutes later we were climbing the stairs to our pensione. We were greeted at the door by Aunt Estelle, who listened to our news about Caitlin's true identity with a slightly distracted look. When Bess got to the part about Caitlin staying with us for another night, a shadow crossed Aunt Estelle's face.

"Nancy, dear, may I speak to you for a moment?" she said when everyone was talking about something else.

"Of course," I said, wondering. I followed Aunt Estelle into the spacious tiled kitchen.

"My dear, this is an awkward thing to say, but I suspect that Caitlin has taken something that doesn't belong to her," Aunt Estelle said in a low voice, once I'd closed the kitchen door.

My heart sank. "Are you serious?"

"I'm afraid so. Ugo had a small sketch hanging on the wall in the foyer. A Tiepolo."

I flashed on Caitlin studying the charcoal sketch of the woman's face. She'd identified it as a Tiepolo—and said it was valuable!

"It was there last night, I remember looking at it as we left for our dinner party," Aunt Estelle continued. "But it was missing this morning. Given what Bess and George told me about the circumstances under which you met Caitlin, the logical suspicion is that she made off with it."

I reached up and pinched the skin between my eyebrows. I was starting to get a headache.

"If she has it, I'll get it back," I promised. "I'm really sorry, Aunt Estelle."

"It's not your fault, dear," she said. "It's clear that the poor girl has some sort of problem. But unfortunately under the circumstances I'm afraid I can't allow her to stay here for another night. It would be one thing if she'd taken something of mine, but I cannot have Ugo's hospitality so abused. I'm sorry."

"Don't be," I said grimly. "You're absolutely right."

Fuming, I marched out to the living room and took Caitlin's arm. Steering her into the bedroom we shared, I demanded, "Where's the Tiepolo?"

"Where's the what?" Caitlin's eyes were pools of innocence.

"Don't pull that act with me," I snapped, resisting the urge to shake her. "I know you took it. You were looking at it last night, you knew it was valuable, and now it's gone. You steal things. What other conclusion could I possibly come to?"

"I don't know! Stop it, you're hurting my arm," Caitlin said. Her eyes had filled with tears and her chin was wobbling. "I can't believe you think I took that drawing!"

In answer I grabbed her handbag and dumped it out on my bed. "Hey!" she protested. I ignored her.

A hairbrush and a makeup bag fell out, with assorted other small things. And a small, square package wrapped in newspaper. I picked it up and tore away the newspaper covering.

There in my hands was the missing Tiepolo sketch.

I glared at Caitlin, who looked like a trapped animal. "How could you? After all we did for you. After Aunt Estelle let you stay here when she'd never even met you before. How could you repay her kindness like this?"

"I'm sorry!" she wailed, and burst into tears. "I'm so sorry!

"I don't know why I did it. You're right, it was a horrible thing to do," she said between sobs. "I just—I just couldn't help it. It was there, and I knew I could get a lot for it, and it was just so . . . so *easy*. I'm sorry, I'm sorry!"

"Don't apologize to me, apologize to Aunt Estelle," I told her. "And get your stuff together. I'm taking you back to your place. You can't stay here anymore."

"My place?" she gasped. "But you said—I can't go back there! They'll come for me!"

Not my problem, I felt like saying. But it was my problem. I'd seen with my own eyes that someone really was after Caitlin. I couldn't leave her alone.

"I'm coming with you," I said. Under the circumstances it was the last thing I wanted to do, but there was no way around it.

I packed an overnight bag for myself. In silence we left the pensione, boarded the Metro yet again, and rode up north. I took Caitlin back to the American Embassy, where we visited Mr. Lutz and got him to send official e-mails to Caitlin's parents, notifying them that she'd lost her memory and needed a family member to come help her. Then we headed to Caitlin's rented room.

The sun, which had never really made an appearance that day, was low in the sky by the time we got there. Caitlin produced the spare key Signora Alberti had given her and we entered the house. Signora Alberti didn't appear to be home—no one answered when I called out a hello—so we headed across the shadowy courtyard to Caitlin's room.

I was still furious with Caitlin. She obviously knew

it, because she kept alternating between bursts of nervous chatter and guilty silence. "Oh, that's funny, we must have left the door open when . . ."

She trailed off as I waved her to silence. All my senses were instantly alert. I had a clear memory of pulling the door closed behind me when we'd left earlier that day. Now it was ajar. Of course, Signora Alberti could have opened it after we were gone, but I wasn't taking any chances.

I gestured to Caitlin to move back. "Go into the main house," I mouthed to her. "Hide!"

Her face was sheet white, but she nodded and hurried across the courtyard.

Moving noiselessly, I pushed open the door just enough to slip inside. I paused a moment as my eyes adjusted to the gloom.

The tiniest whisper of sound to my left—maybe a shoe, scraping ever so slightly against the tiled floor—warned me. I spun and caught a blur of movement coming toward me. I ducked and rolled. A hand swung through the air where I had been a moment ago.

A hand clutching something that flashed silver.

A knife!

CHAPTER **14**

FRANK

A SEA OF SECRETS

By the time we started back toward our room at the university, I think my face had turned from bright red back to its normal color. I still felt like an idiot, though.

"Dude, Nancy was totally flirting with you!" Joe had said to me as soon as the girls were out of sight.

"She wasn't flirting. She was teasing me," I muttered. This was *not* something I wanted to discuss with Joe right now—or ever, in fact.

"Same thing, man. Didn't you notice the way she took your arm and all? She's into you," Joe insisted.

"She has a boyfriend already," I pointed out. "Anyway, we're just friends. Drop it, all right?"

"If you say so," Joe said, but he gave me a knowing

grin. I resisted the urge to smack him on the side of his head.

"Let's figure out our next moves," I said. "I'm going to get in touch with ATAC and pass on everything that we've learned so far. And I'll see if they've dug up any other leads for us. I think I'll go back to the dorm room to do that—writing long e-mails on this little phone keypad is too much of a pain."

"I'm going with you to the room to pick up some supplies. Then I'll head back down to BS and T," Joe said promptly. "Whatever happened to Caitlin and Sam, there's some connection to that place. Maybe if I poke around some I can figure out what it is."

"What kind of supplies do you need?" I asked, puzzled.

Joe smirked. "Doggy tranquilizers. I'm pretty sure we have some in our ATAC emergency packs. Forewarned is forearmed—I don't want to fight off rottweilers like you had to."

"Good plan," I admitted. "All right, let's do it."

So now here I was, booting up the computer. Joe had just left, taking with him a backpack containing the dog tranquilizers and a few other things that might come in handy, like a high-powered flashlight and a small crowbar.

I went online and checked my e-mail. There were two messages there from ATAC. The first one simply said that Caitlin Boggs's juvenile arrest had been for shoplifting as Joe had predicted. No surprise there.

The second message contained information about Claude Bonaire, our billionaire dig sponsor and shipping company owner. I skimmed through it.

Bonaire, it seemed, was truly obsessed with Emperor Claudius. He'd even written a book about Claudius, called *Playing the Fool*. An excerpt from the flap copy promised that the book would "lay to rest once and for all the notion that Claudius was anything but the most brilliant ruler of the Julio-Claudian Dynasty."

"Ooookay," I muttered. Talk about single focus.

There was also a copy of a long feature article from Claude Bonaire's hometown newspaper. He came from a little town in coastal Texas, and clearly he was one of their most illustrious sons. The article detailed his astounding success at building BS&T, and then talked about his scholarly achievements—meaning the book about Claudius.

But the interesting bit came near the end of the article. That's where I read the description of a villa Bonaire was building for himself, apparently in the ancient Roman style (though it would have modern conveniences like electricity and a satellite hookup). It was being constructed on a small uninhabited island Bonaire had bought in the Mediterranean Sea, about ninety miles west of Rome.

The first thing that struck my attention was the small inset map of the area. It showed that Bonaire's island was only about forty or fifty miles away from Corsica. I wasn't sure what the connection was, but I strongly suspected it wasn't coincidence that Corsica kept popping up everywhere we looked.

The second thing that struck me was the layout of Bonaire's villa. The paper had published one of the architect's renderings, which was an aerial view. As I stared at it I realized that I was looking at a building layout that I'd seen before. Yesterday, to be exact.

Bonaire was constructing an exact replica of Claudius's Emerald Bower.

I let out a long, low whistle and leaned back in my desk chair. "That's interesting," I murmured. "Very, very interesting."

A crazy idea was forming in my mind. Maybe the theft of artifacts we'd been sent to investigate wasn't entirely a dead issue yet. Maybe it was just happening for completely different reasons and being committed by completely different people from what we'd thought.

Claude Bonaire was obsessed with Emperor Claudius—to the extent, apparently, that he'd had a family tree done showing that he was Claudius's descendant.

What if, in his mind, that meant he was entitled to

some of Claudius's things? Especially things that would look good in the replica of Claudius's house he was building? Things that would make it even more authentic?

I thought of the emerald-eyed lions that no one had found at the dig. "I bet I know where those are," I said aloud.

Turning back to my computer, I began to type in the search bar. I was hunting for a place near Rome that would rent me a fast boat.

There was a Mediterranean island I wanted to pay a visit to. . . .

JOE

By the time I arrived at Civitavecchia, it was after five o'clock, and the offices of BS&T were dark. I was disappointed to see that iron security gates had been pulled closed over the warehouse bays. These guys weren't working late, apparently.

I'd noticed this morning that the warehouse backed onto a wharf where ships could berth to pick up cargo. If I couldn't get into the warehouse, maybe I could check out some of the BS&T cargo ships—there was a possibility I'd learn something. A slim possibility, admittedly, but still better than nothing.

I strolled down to the waterfront, camera in hand, doing my best impression of a clueless tourist. I wandered along the line of docked cargo ships, stopping every now and then to take a picture. The ships were all sizes, some of them enormous, with sides that towered high above my head. The area was still busy, with cranes unloading truck-size containers and forklifts moving smaller cargoes from place to place. The whole place smelled like diesel fuel and fish.

As I walked, I kept an eye out for the BS&T logo. At last, near the end of a pier populated by smaller ships, I spotted it painted on the hull of an elderly-looking vessel with red and black trim. The ship had a raised cabin at the front, with twin stacks that were belching black smoke. A metal gangplank led from the ship to the pier.

I checked the ships on either side. Neither was BS&T. This one appeared to be the only one currently docked here. Which meant it was my target.

From where I stood, I could see that there were men moving about aboard the ship. There was no way I could come up with a good cover story that would get me aboard. I'd have to sneak.

I glanced around me. The ship was moored by thick chains fore and aft. I smiled to myself as I noted that the aft chain came out the side of the ship directly over an open porthole. Even better, a big stack of cargo containers sat on the dock directly in front of that porthole, hiding it and most of the chain from view, unless you happened to be standing where I was standing now.

"That's my way in," I said softly. It would be risky, but that only made it more exciting.

Moving casually, I strolled over to the stack of containers and bent down as if to tie my shoe. First I checked to make sure no one was watching. Then I ducked into the shadow of the containers. Grasping the thick, slime-coated chain in both hands, I swung myself along it hand over hand, working my way toward the porthole.

Voices on the dock made me stop. I strained to peer over my shoulder. A couple of men were walking toward the BS&T ship. I winced as they stopped right next to the stack of containers. One of them, a guy in dirty jeans and a work shirt, was waving his hands in the air and speaking rapidly to the other, who was wearing fatigues and looked more like a military type than a dock worker. I guessed they were having an argument.

I rolled my eyes. "Can't we all just get along?" I said under my breath. If either of them happened to look to the side, they'd spot me.

I hung by my arms, dangling over the water without moving, for what felt like ten minutes while the two men argued. Finally the guy in fatigues threw up his hands and stomped away. The dock worker followed, still haranguing him. Letting out my breath, I continued on my way.

My shoulder muscles were burning by the time I got within three feet of the side of the ship. Gritting my teeth, I swung my legs up to wrap them around the chain. My plan was to hang by my legs and swing myself in at the open porthole.

I dangled there for a moment like a spider on a web, gathering my strength. My head was lower than my feet.

"Now comes the hard part," I muttered. Taking a deep breath, I let go of the chain with my hands and swung forward, reaching for the lip of the porthole. Missed! As I swung back for a second try, out of the corner of my eye, I spotted something small shooting out of one of the side pockets of my backpack and splashing into the ocean. Oh, well. Whatever it was, I hoped it wasn't important.

As I arced forward, I strained to reach forward, scrabbling for a handhold. My fingers closed on a raised metal sill. Yes! "Got it!" I grunted softly.

Holding tight with my left hand, I reached inside as far as I could and grasped a metal bar on the inside of the ship. I pulled myself as far in as I could, then let go with my legs.

For a moment I hung half in and half out of the porthole. I wriggled forward. The porthole was small, and with my backpack on my back it seemed for a moment like I wasn't going to be able to squeeze through, but then I gave a mighty heave forward, heard a ripping sound, and felt something give. I slid the rest of the way inside headfirst.

I scrambled quickly to my feet, crouching in a defensive pose in case I'd entered a cabin that was occupied. But as my eyes adjusted to the dimness, I saw that I was alone. I was in what looked like a cargo hold of some kind—just a big, mostly empty space with stuff stacked at the far end. I couldn't see exactly what it was in the limited light.

The whole ship vibrated slightly, and there was a faint, deep rumble that filled the air. The engines must be running, I guessed.

I checked my backpack to see what had ripped, but I couldn't find anything. Then, glancing down, I noticed the mangled front pocket of my jeans. "Oh, man," I grumbled softly. They were my favorite jeans, too!

The nice thing about the engine running was that it would provide good cover for any noises I might make. The bad thing was that I'd have to be extra alert, since I probably wouldn't hear anyone coming up behind me.

I moved forward slowly, checking frequently over my shoulder. I held my flashlight loosely in one hand and my crowbar in the other. Either one could serve as a weapon if I needed them. Handy!

As I drew closer, I saw that the cargo stacked at the far end of the hold was mixed. There were several palettes of thick, curved red tiles, each about eight inches square. I stared at them for a moment in puzzlement until I realized what they were. Roofing tiles! Terra-cotta roofing tiles, just like the tiles on practically every roof in Rome.

Next to the roofing tiles were more palettes, these stacked with big rectangular slabs of a grayish white stone that I was pretty sure was unpolished marble.

Okay. So the BS&T ship was carrying building materials. "Highly suspicious," I muttered under my breath. *Not.*

My pulse sped up as a door swung open somewhere to my left, spilling yellow light into the dim hold. I scrambled behind the palettes of marble, holding my breath.

Voices came toward me, and when I peeked through a gap in the palettes I saw that one of the speakers was my old buddy, the guy in the work shirt from the dock. Fatigues guy was with him again, as well as two more people—another guy in fatigues, and Joanna Paoli.

Hmmm. . . .

The two fatigues guys were carrying a medium-size box between them. From what I could make out in the dim light, it looked high tech and high security, made of some silvery metal—maybe titanium. It had carry handles on either side.

The one in the work shirt was still lecturing, jabbing the air with his finger as he made his point. Joanna had a scowl on her face.

Both of the guys in fatigues, I noticed with sudden intense interest, had the same rectangular patch sewed to the breast of their uniform shirt: a white patch with a black head in silhouette in the middle of it.

The Corsican flag again. The way it was sewn onto their fatigues, it looked like a uniform—the uniform of the Corsican Army. But from what Frank and I had learned about Corsica, there was no Corsican Army.

Or was there?

Joanna pointed to the palettes of roof tiles and asked work-shirt guy something. Work-shirt guy shook his head violently and pointed at the roof. *"Deve rimanere fuori,"* he snapped. *"E' pericolosa."*

Whatever that meant.

"Bah!" growled Joanna, throwing up her hands. She beckoned to the two fatigue-clad guys, spun, and headed for the door. *"Andiamo!"* she shouted over her shoulder. That word I recognized from old mobster movies. It meant "let's go."

The guys fell in obediently behind her, carrying the box as gingerly as if it contained a cargo of live cobras. *What could be in there?* I wondered. I didn't know how, but I was going to find out before I left the ship.

Work-shirt guy shrugged and followed. It was pretty clear he'd won the argument.

As he was walking out, work-shirt guy noticed the open porthole. Crossing to it, he stopped to close and latch it. I crossed my fingers, hoping I hadn't dropped anything there. But he didn't seem to notice anything amiss. A moment later he left the hold and the door swung closed behind him.

As soon as I was sure they were gone, I swung my pack off my shoulders and started rooting through it for my phone. I wanted to update Frank on what I'd seen and where I was.

But where was my phone? It wasn't in the side pocket where I thought I'd left it. I checked all the other pockets, but it wasn't there. Scowling, I dumped everything out onto the floor.

As I searched through my stuff, I was vaguely aware of a rattling and clanking going on somewhere on the ship. But I didn't really pay attention. I was more concerned with finding my phone. Which wasn't anywhere in my pack.

At that point I had a sudden flash of myself swinging from the chain outside the porthole and the small object falling into the sea below me. My phone!

"Oh, man," I groaned. It had been something important after all.

ATAC wouldn't be happy. They gave us lots of cool equipment, but somehow they expected that we would give it back to them at the end of the mission, as good as new. Of course that rarely happened. The way I approached my missions, things like cool spy gadgets tended to get a little mangled. Which made ATAC cranky.

This was going to make them extra cranky.

PHWOOOOM! I jumped as, with a roar, the ship's engines revved up. Whoa! Were we going somewhere?

I staggered as the big craft jerked into motion. We surged forward. Regaining my balance, I ran to the porthole I'd climbed in. To my dismay I saw that we were already about twenty yards away from the dock, and the distance was growing rapidly. That clanking sound I'd heard must have been the docking chains being hauled in.

I pressed my nose against the porthole, wondering if I could jump out and swim back to the dock. But one look at the churning white water in the ship's wake told me that was a no-go. The propeller screws were at the rear, and if I jumped in anywhere near them, I'd be sucked in and chopped up into tiny bits. A nice treat for any nearby sharks, yes, but not so good for my health.

"Okay," I said aloud, "let's assess the situation." Here I was, stowed away on a ship going who knows where, crewed by people who were probably hostile and possibly criminal. I had no phone, no way to contact Frank, and no one knew where I was.

Oh yeah, and, I realized all of a sudden, I was *starving*.

"Great!" I clapped my hands together. "What else could possibly go wrong?"

CHAPTER *15*

A BROTHER VANISHES

I sprang into a crouch, my eyes fixed on the gleaming blade that had just missed giving me a haircut. Adrenaline surged through me.

The guy holding it, I could see now, was the same one who'd chased Caitlin and me earlier that day—a hulking man with dark hair combed back from his forehead and deep-set eyes.

Those eyes widened as they focused on me. *"No é la ragazza!"* he growled.

I understood enough to gather that he'd been expecting Caitlin, not me. I seized the moment of surprise and hurled myself at his knife hand. Grabbing his wrist, I sank my teeth into it—a short, sharp chomp.

He howled and the knife clattered to the floor. Before

he could do anything, I kicked it as hard as I could. It skittered across the tiles and under a large wardrobe.

There! At least the odds were slightly less against me now.

An instant later the man regained his senses and swung his free hand at the side of my head. I saw it coming and twisted away, but even so, the blow was hard enough to make me see stars. I gasped and stumbled back.

He loomed over me. *"Dove la ragazza?"* he demanded. *Where is the girl?*

"Con la polizia!" I lied. *With the police.*

His face twisted in anger and he lunged for me with his hands outstretched. I scrambled backward, putting a massive wooden chair between me and him, and shoved it at him. It caught him in the knees.

"Aiiii!" he snarled. My heart constricted. The look on his face was truly murderous now.

At that moment there came a miraculous sound. Police sirens. They had that funny, tinny tone that European police sirens do, but it was still the most beautiful sound I'd heard in a long time.

My mind whirred. Of course, the police weren't coming to *my* aid. They just happened to be responding to some other emergency nearby—a fact the attacker would realize if he waited. But could I make him too afraid to wait?

My attacker paused, his head raised. Uncertainty warred with anger on his face.

"*La polizia,*" I said, making my voice as confident as I could. I gave him a taunting smile, though inside I was shaking.

He glared at me for a long moment. *Oh, no! Did I push it too far?* I thought.

Then, with a wordless growl, he turned and ran out the door. I hurried to the doorway and saw him career through Signora Alberti's house. I hoped Caitlin had hidden herself well.

I let two minutes pass while I caught my breath and waited for my knees to stop shaking. Then I crossed the courtyard. "Caitlin?" I called. "It's safe now. You can come out."

Another two minutes passed before she finally emerged from the kitchen door. Her eyes grew enormous as she took in my disheveled appearance.

"Are you okay?" she quavered.

"Mostly," I assured her, though the side of my head throbbed where the goon had hit me. I'd have a bruise for sure.

"Oh my gosh, Nancy, I can't believe it. They really did come for me," she babbled. "Why? What did I do? What do they want?" She was on the verge of hysteria.

"I don't know yet," I said grimly, "but I'm absolutely going to find out. There's no way I'm dropping this case now. They messed with the wrong girl!" Now that the danger was over, reaction was setting in and I was steaming mad.

"But what are we going to do now? Where are we going to go? We're not safe anywhere!" Caitlin wailed.

I paused, realizing she had a point. Maybe we should go to the police. Much as I wanted to see this case through to the end, maybe it was just too dangerous.

Then the answer came to me. The bad guys might have thugs with knives, but we had a couple of secret agents with cool spy gadgets on our side.

"We'll be safe with Frank and Joe," I said. "Come on, let's go."

By the time we emerged from the Metro stop near the university where Frank and Joe were staying, it was fully dark. My head was aching fiercely from the blow I'd taken, and Caitlin looked white and exhausted.

I'd called Frank from a pay phone to ask if we could come, and he'd given me directions. He was waiting for us by the front gate of the university, and ushered us past the security guards and into his dorm.

"Are you sure you're all right?" he asked, handing me a bottle of cold fruit juice. "Maybe we should get you to a hospital to make sure you don't have a concussion. Blows to the head can be serious."

"I didn't black out," I assured him. I pressed the chilled bottle against the tender spot on my scalp. "I'm just tired and in pain, that's all. And I'm really, really mad."

Frank studied me with his head cocked. A grin spread across his face. "Yeah, I can see that," he said.

Caitlin and I filled him in on our afternoon's adventure, and then he brought me up to date on what he and Joe had been doing since lunch. "Joe was snooping around BS and T some more. To tell the truth, I'm getting a little worried about him," he said, rubbing the back of his neck. "I called his cell a couple of times and he hasn't answered. Now, he's not the best at staying in touch, but still, I thought he'd be back by now. He's been gone almost six hours."

"And there's no way you can track him?" I asked. "I figured ATAC would have given you homing devices, with all the gadgets you have."

"They did," Frank said. "Our phones have homing beacons. But they have to be activated to transmit, and Joe's isn't."

"Maybe that means he's not in trouble," I suggested.

"I hope so," Frank agreed, but I could see by his eyes that he wasn't totally convinced.

Caitlin curled up on Joe's bed and listened silently while Frank and I talked over our case. He told me what he'd learned about Claude Bonaire, the billionaire amateur archaeologist. He showed me the article about Bonaire's replica of the Emerald Bower.

"I've arranged to rent a speedboat from Civitavecchia in the morning. I want to go check out this replica," Frank said. "The island it's on is right near here, and it's also close to Corsica, as you can see from the map. I have a feeling that we might find some answers there."

"Can you drive a speedboat?" I asked.

"I've done it a few times," he said. "Joe's the one who really loves those things." He fell silent, drumming his fingers nervously on the table. I knew what was going through his mind.

"Is there any other way we could track Joe?" I asked. "Maybe ATAC knows how to pinpoint his phone even without the homing beacon activated."

Frank nodded. "It's worth asking," he agreed. Picking up his phone, he stood up. "Sorry, but I'm going to have to make this call in private," he said. "It's one of the strictest rules they have, that we never use our emergency contact number when anyone else is around, no matter who."

I nodded. It made sense.

Frank left the room. A few moments later he came back in. "That was a good idea you had," he told me. "ATAC does track the location of each of its phones continuously, as long as the phone is switched on.

They're going to get back to me as soon as they have anything."

"Great!" I exclaimed.

"In the meantime," he said with a smile, "I could use something to eat, and I'm guessing you two could also."

Frank had gone out and bought a loaf of fresh bread, some cheese, and some fruit while he waited for Caitlin and me. We feasted on this, washing it all down with bottles of sparkling water. By the time we finished, I felt ten times better than I had, and Caitlin's cheeks had some color in them again.

"There's just something about Italian bread," I said, brushing crumbs from the table into my cupped hand. "It's the best-tasting bread in the world."

Frank's phone rang and he grabbed it eagerly. "Hello?"

I watched as he listened for a moment. "Right," he said. His eager look faded, to be replaced by one of growing concern. "Right. . . . I see. . . . Got it. Okay, thanks."

He flipped the phone closed and sat there for a moment. His lips were compressed into a tight line of worry.

"Tell me," I said, putting a hand on his arm.

"Joe's phone was broadcasting all day, which means at least he had it turned on," Frank replied. "My contact checked the records, and since about five twenty, it was broadcasting from one location. My contact pinpointed this location as about five yards west of a dock in Civitavecchia."

I frowned as I tried to picture this. "Five yards *west* of a dock? But doesn't that mean it's . . ."

"In the water, yes," Frank confirmed, nodding. "Twenty feet under, in fact. The satellite can measure depths. The phone was there, not moving, until it stopped broadcasting at about six thirty."

"Could it have run out of battery?" Caitlin asked.

Frank shrugged. "It's possible. But the point is, before it stopped broadcasting it was there, under water, for more than an hour." He looked wretched.

"That doesn't mean that Joe was there with it," I said quickly. "Maybe he just dropped his phone. Come on, Frank, your brother is a smart and resourceful guy. He's going to be okay. You have to believe that."

"You're right," Frank said, brightening slightly. "He is resourceful. He's also incredibly careless with his stuff. I bet he *did* drop his phone."

"Do you want to go there now and check it out?" I asked. "I'll go with you if you do."

Frank was already online, checking train schedules. A moment later he shook his head. "There are no trains to Civitavecchia at this time of night," he said. "The next one is at five tomorrow morning." He smacked his hand down on the desk. "I feel so helpless!"

"We'll be on that train," I told him. "We'll go there and we'll find him, Frank. Believe it."

Closing his eyes, he took a deep breath. "Okay. You're right. I've just got to think positive. What else can I do?"

"You can try to get some sleep," I suggested. "I know it won't be easy, but the more rest you get, the better able you'll be to deal with whatever we find there."

Frank opened his eyes and gave me a crooked smile. "Right again. Thanks, Nancy."

I smiled back, feeling a rush of warmth for him. "Any time. Now lie down and get some rest."

He did as I told him, stretching out fully clothed on his bed. Caitlin was on Joe's bed, so I made myself as comfortable as I could on a small couch. Then I turned the lights out and we all lay there, silent in the darkness—waiting for the dawn.

CHAPTER *16*

FRANK

SCOUTING BY SEA

I didn't think I'd be able to sleep at all, but I must have dozed off for a couple of hours, because I woke up to find Nancy bending over me, gently shaking my shoulder. "Wake up," she was saying. "It's time."

Time for what? I gazed up at her, dazed with sleep. "You're pretty," I mumbled.

She smiled. "Why, thank you!"

Suddenly I realized what I'd said. *That* brought me awake in a hurry. I sat up fast and swung my legs over the edge of my bed, avoiding Nancy's gaze. My face was burning.

I cleared my throat. "I'll, uh . . . I'll just go—I mean, I've got to—"

"Right," Nancy said quickly. "You go ahead."

As I hurried out of the room I heard Caitlin saying, "He has to do what? What was he talking about?"

I thought of how Joe would have made fun of me, and that made me remember with a fresh jolt of worry that Joe was missing. *He* was the reason we were up so early. We were heading to Civitavecchia to find him.

I hurried down the hall to the communal dormitory bathroom. Turning on the cold water, I splashed my face and neck vigorously, wetting my hair and shaking it dry. After I brushed my teeth, I was ready to face the day.

Nancy, Caitlin, and I left the dorm and caught the Metro to the train station. We made it with ten minutes to spare, so Nancy and Caitlin went off and got us coffee and rolls for the ride while I got tickets. Then we all boarded the Civitavecchia train. This was getting to be a bad habit, I thought.

In spite of myself, though, I couldn't help admiring the sunrise that greeted us as we stepped off the train. The normally busy port town was hushed and silent, and early light sparkled on the wavelets of the Mediterranean. The sky was cloudless, the air calm—it looked like a perfect day.

Using the satellite coordinate that my ATAC contact had sent to my phone, I led the girls down to the docks by the BS&T offices. The spot that Joe's phone had broadcast its last pings from was about two-thirds of the way along a pier reserved for smaller cargo ships and fishing boats. There was nothing moored there, though there were ships on either side of the spot.

A few fishermen were walking around, getting ready to go out for the day, and between us, Nancy and I were able to ask one of them if there'd been a ship moored there yesterday afternoon. He squinted off at the horizon, thinking, and then said, *"Si, si. L'Olivino. Bay essay tay."*

It took me a moment to translate that into my mind into "BST." My heart leaped. There'd been a BS&T ship in this spot!

"Do you think he got on that ship somehow?" Nancy asked me in a low voice.

"I think it's a good possibility," I replied. "The question is, why? And where was it going?"

Nancy turned back to the fisherman and, with a lot of pausing and sign language, asked if he had any idea where the *Olivino* was bound. But he shook his head.

"Non so," he said sadly. *I don't know. "Ma cerca, cerca. L'Olivino é piu piccolo, piu vecchio."* And he reeled off a long declaration that neither Nancy nor I understood. But I didn't really need to, because I'd understood the important thing: the *Olivino* was small and old, and therefore made only local trips.

So it had to be somewhere close by. And that meant, with luck, Joe was close by too.

The only place I could think of that was nearby and was connected to BS&T was the island owned by Claude Bonaire. The one off the Corsican coast. So that was the place I would go.

"Who's up for a speedboat ride?" I asked.

Two hours later I throttled the engine of the speedboat back to a low growl. "There it is," I said, pointing. "Claude Bonaire's private island."

Ahead of us lay a small, mountainous island, maybe a mile long. The shore that faced us was a cliff, rising about fifty feet out of the water. Seabirds wheeled at its base, and at the top grew scraggly pines and cypress trees. There was no sign of human habitation.

"Are you sure it's the right one?" Nancy asked. We'd passed two other small islands in the past fifteen minutes.

"According to the GPS coordinates that ATAC gave me, this is the one," I replied.

I edged the powerful speedboat closer in, keeping the engine low so as to maintain control. We'd lucked out in getting this boat—or rather ATAC had been able to pull some strings for us. My contact had directed us to a local boat dealer who let us take one of his most expensive models. It was a long, sleek boat with a sharp nose and tons of horsepower—it had done sixty miles an hour for ninety minutes with no problem at all, and

I had a feeling I could have pushed it a lot faster. But I'd wanted to reach the island in one piece.

Nancy was studying the satellite photo I'd downloaded onto my laptop. I'd brought it with me for the day so I could be in fuller contact with ATAC if I needed to. So far it was proving to be a wise decision.

"It looks like there's a decent-size natural harbor around the north end," she said to me. "That's probably where the ship went, if it's here."

"Let's check it out," I said, turning the nose of the boat around.

"Why are we going back out to sea?" Caitlin asked in a plaintive voice. "I was hoping we could go ashore. I don't feel very well."

I was about to explain, but Nancy beat me to it. "We can't go ashore until we scout out the island and find the safest place to land," she said. "We need to stay far out for two reasons. One, we don't know what kind of hidden rocks there might be close in shore. Two, we don't want anyone who might be on the island to see us and wonder what we're doing snooping around. We need to be far enough away that we don't seem suspicious."

Exactly what I would have said. It wasn't the first time today that I'd been struck by how much Nancy and I thought alike.

Still keeping the engine speed low, I turned the

speedboat north and cruised parallel to the shore. Ahead of us I could see where it curved away to the left. Nancy angled the computer screen so that I could see it and pointed out the angle of the harbor on the photo.

"See, there's the headland there, and on the other side there's a bay. It looks like there's been some kind of seawall built here." She traced her finger along a white ridge that ran southwest to northeast through the shallow water at the island's north end.

"Got it." I turned the wheel gently to the left and the boat curved around the island, leaving a long white wake behind it.

"I see a ship at a dock in there!" Nancy announced a moment later. "Hand me the binoculars, Caitlin."

I slowed down as much as I dared while Nancy studied the vessel. From this distance I could see that it had a brick red hull with a black stripe, and a raised cabin with two smokestacks at the front end. It was moored at a floating dock that ran out a good ways into the little bay. That must be the spot where the water was deep enough that the ship wouldn't run aground.

"I can't . . . quite . . . make out the name on the side," Nancy said, not taking the binoculars from her eyes. "Frank, do you think you can get us in a little closer?"

"I'll try," I said, and I began turning the wheel.

"Let me see those," Caitlin said suddenly. She snatched the binoculars out of Nancy's grasp so urgently that Nancy barely had time to disentangle her hand from the nylon strap.

"Hey!" Nancy protested. "Where's the fire?"

Caitlin didn't answer. She was gazing intently through the binoculars. A second later she dropped them with a clatter onto the deck. Her voice was strangled as she said, "Turn around!"

"What?" I said, startled.

"Turn around! Turn around now!" Caitlin insisted. "We have to get out of here!"

"Why?" Nancy asked quickly. "What's wrong, Caitlin?"

But Caitlin had gone beyond reason. With a moan of fear, she climbed up onto the cushioned seat of the speedboat. Then, while Nancy and I gaped at her in complete bewilderment, she dove over the side of the boat—into the open sea!

ISLAND ADVENTURE

"Caitlin!" I cried, lunging to grab hold of her. But it was too late. My fingers closed on air.

Caitlin bobbed up after a moment, already ten feet behind us. Her face was white and shocked, and her mouth opened soundlessly. A second later she went under again.

"Take the wheel!" Frank ordered. He was already kicking off his shoes. "I'll go after her."

When I hesitated, he said, "I've done my share of lifeguarding in the summers. And you shouldn't be too active with that bump on your head."

He had a point. Sliding over, I grasped the wheel. Pausing only to pull his T-shirt over his head, Frank dove cleanly into the water.

For a moment I focused on steering the boat, shoving the throttle almost into idle. I made a wide circle back toward where we'd been a few seconds ago.

Frank had reached Caitlin already. He'd wrapped one arm around her from behind and was swimming strongly with the other. I reversed gear to stop the boat's forward motion. Then I cut the engine altogether, not wanting to risk either of them getting tangled in the propellers.

When Frank swam alongside the boat, I was ready with a life ring on a rope. I tossed it to him and he wrapped it around Caitlin's waist. She swayed limply in the water, but I could see that she was conscious.

Puffing and panting, we managed to hoist her up over the side. She slid onto the stern cushions and lay there in a shivering heap. Frank pulled himself up after her, his wet brown arms glistening in the morning sun.

He sat for a moment with his head down, catching his breath. Then he looked up and gave me a lopsided grin. "Nice driving," he commented.

"Nice lifeguarding," I replied with an answering smile.

Both of us turned to regard Caitlin, whose teeth had begun to chatter. "What was that all about?" I asked her. "We're in the middle of the Mediterranean Sea! What were you thinking, Caitlin?"

"Th-th-that sh-sh-sh-ship," Caitlin managed. "I

re-re-re-recognize it. Th-that's where I was being held p-prisoner when I was m-m-m-missing."

A jolt of excitement shot through me. "You remember?"

Caitlin nodded. "I r-remember it all," she said. She gave a convulsive shudder. "I'm so c-c-cold! My teeth are ch-ch-ch-chattering s-so hard, I c-c-can't t-talk. Aren't there any t-towels on this boat?"

"Um . . . no," I said, resisting the urge to point out that (a) it was a rental boat, and (b) no one had told her to go jumping into the ocean anyway. "Sorry. Lie down on the cushions. You'll be out of the wind and the sun will dry you pretty fast."

Frank, meanwhile, had put his T-shirt back on and restarted the engine. We motored away around the west side of the island. "I don't want anyone wondering why we're hanging around," he explained. "It's pretty clear that we need to go ashore here. So let's find a cove or something where we can pull in, and then once we're all set, Caitlin can tell us what she remembers."

"Good idea," I agreed.

The shore along this side was rocky, but it wasn't a sheer cliff like the east side. From the satellite photo, it didn't seem like there were any inlets, but it was hard to tell. I stood in the bow of the boat with the binoculars, scanning the shoreline as Frank drove slowly south.

"Hey, what about over there?" I said, pointing at what looked like a dent in the shoreline. Past the rocks, I'd caught a glimpse of what looked like a sandy beach.

Frank turned the nose of the boat toward the island, and we glided in. As we got close he cut the power to almost nothing. I stood at the bow, keeping a sharp eye out for submerged rocks that might rip our hull.

"Go left," I called back. "A little more. Now straighten it out. Good—whoa! Hard right!" We were about to run onto a sharp rock that I hadn't seen until the last moment.

Luckily Frank was really good at maneuvering the speedboat, and we squeaked by the rock with about an inch to spare. We glided forward, through a skinny passage lined with boulders, then under an arch of overhanging trees, and suddenly we were in a beautiful little cove with a sandy bottom. Best of all, it was almost completely hidden, both from above by the canopy of trees, and from the sea by its narrow, rocky inlet.

"Perfect," Frank said, giving me a high five. I took off my shoes, then jumped over the side into the shallow water with the painter rope in my hand. I waded ashore and tied the rope around a big boulder at the water's edge.

Frank was already helping Caitlin over the side. She splashed onto the beach, looking like a half-drowned rat, and sat down in a patch of sun.

I sat facing her. "Okay, tell us everything you can," I said.

"Who put you in that ship, and why?" Frank added.

"It was Joanna Paoli," Caitlin said. She'd finally stopped shivering. "But I have no idea why. I never knew why. All I know is, Sam and I went into the BS and T warehouse one night. He'd come to get some crates for the dig, and I was helping him get them. And I wanted to show him something." She gave me a guilty look from under her lashes. "I'd put aside a crate of stuff that I thought would be easy to take and easy to sell. I tried to talk him into it. But he wouldn't do it. We had . . . well, kind of a fight, and I started to cry and ran off. I wasn't looking where I was going and I guess I went the wrong way, because all of a sudden I came around a corner and there were a bunch of men in army clothes, gathered around a bunch of boxes."

"Army clothes like what the guy who chased us was wearing?" I asked.

Caitlin nodded. "With that symbol—the black head on the white background."

"They must be Corsican separatists," Frank said to me. "From what I know, there are apparently a few different separatist groups, but none of the ones that are currently active are violent. The last violent separatist group fell apart in the eighties."

"What happened next?" I asked Caitlin.

"When they saw me they got really mad," Caitlin replied. "They started yelling at me, but they were talking in Italian and I didn't understand." She swallowed hard. "Then one of them grabbed me and pulled out a gun. I thought he was going to shoot me! I screamed out, 'Sam! Sam!' After that I think one of them must have hit me, because everything went black for a while."

Frank raised his eyebrows. "A gun, huh? I have a feeling this group might be planning to bring back the bad old days of separatist violence."

"Sounds like it," I had to agree. My stomach contracted. What craziness had we gotten ourselves into here?

"The next thing I remember, I was being carried aboard that ship back there," Caitlin told us. "I was tied up and gagged. They took me down below and Joanna was there, in one of the holds. When I first saw her I thought, *Oh, it's all been a huge mistake. These scary guys are security guards. She'll tell them I work for her and they'll let me go.* But that didn't happen."

"What did?" Frank wanted to know.

"Joanna didn't even say one word to me," Caitlin said. "She just talked to the men. I guess they were telling her how they found me, and she was yelling at them. I'm not sure why. But anyway, finally she made them put me down in this dark, wet, smelly space in the very bottom of the ship." Caitlin shivered. "That was when I realized they were probably planning to kill me. There were r-rats down there, I could feel them running over my legs in the dark. And—and they just left me there, hour after hour. Sometimes someone would bring me food and water. I don't even know how long I was there. It felt like a year." Her eyes welled up with tears. "It was *horrible*."

"Wow, it sure was," I said sympathetically. Talk about an ordeal.

"But you got out somehow," Frank pointed out. "Did you escape?"

Caitlin nodded. "The rats actually helped me," she said. "One day the men gave me a sandwich with some kind of meat in it, and I took a bit of it and rubbed it on the ropes that I was tied with. The rats smelled the meat and nibbled the ropes. Once my hands and legs were free, I snuck off the ship. I was on that dock we were at this morning, in Civitavecchia. And then I tried to call Sam on his cell phone and he didn't answer and didn't answer, and I guess I sort of lost it. And then I don't remember anything until I woke up in the Borghese gardens."

I nodded, my thoughts whirling as I processed what Caitlin had told us.

"So the way I see it," I said, thinking aloud, "Joanna Paoli and her separatist buddies have been using

BS and T as the staging area for whatever violent acts they're planning. It must be pretty easy to smuggle weapons when you control a shipping company."

"Right," Frank agreed. "Caitlin must have walked in on them when they were loading some guns, or something like that. They saw her, they panicked, they took her captive so she couldn't go to the police and tell them what she saw."

"But I didn't see anything!" Caitlin protested. "I didn't see any guns. Just boxes. I have no idea what was in them. It could have been lampshades, for all I know!"

"But they couldn't be sure of that," I told her. "That's why they grabbed you, and that's why they were trying to get you back."

Frank was nodding vigorously. "We're on the right track, I can feel it," he said. "And this island makes an ideal headquarters for a terrorist group. It's uninhabited—and therefore off the authorities' radar—but, because of Claude Bonaire's construction project, there's a legitimate reason for lots of boat traffic in and out. *And* it's close to Corsica. What could be more perfect?"

I got to my feet. "Frank, we have to find out exactly what the separatists are planning," I said urgently. "If they're really going to launch some sort of terrorist attack, we have to stop them!"

"We've also got to find my brother," Frank said. He,

too, was on his feet. "He's somewhere on this island. I just hope he didn't get captured by the separatists."

"Let's get moving," I said.

I turned inland—then froze in my tracks as a voice rang out from the trees. "We've got you surrounded! Put your hands on top of your heads and no one will get hurt!"

CHAPTER **18**

FRANK

THE FINAL SURPRISE

I had a moment of sheer, pulsing adrenaline as I heard the voice telling us to surrender. Then it evaporated, leaving me shaking with reaction.

I knew that voice!

"*Joe!*" I yelled.

And, grinning his maddening, cocky grin, my younger brother stepped out from the trees. His white T-shirt was smeared with mud and his jeans were ripped, but he was all in one piece otherwise.

"Had you going, didn't I?" he said.

"You *idiot*!" I growled. I couldn't figure out whether I wanted to hug him or strangle him. "I was about to tackle you!"

"We've been worried sick about you!" Nancy chimed in.

"You scared me to death!" Caitlin accused him.

Joe held up his hands. "Whoa, sorry, everyone. I guess that was kind of a dirty trick. I just couldn't resist. Sorry."

"Seriously, you don't know how glad I am to see you. I could kiss you all—even Frank, and that's saying something. Hey, you didn't happen to bring any food with you, did you? I haven't eaten since lunch yesterday."

We all stared at him for a moment. Then Caitlin said, "Um, I didn't eat most of my croissant. If you want it, it's on the boat."

"A croissant?" Joe groaned. He splashed out to the boat and retrieved the bakery bag with Caitlin's roll in it. "That's it? I could eat a whole side of beef."

"Joe," I said severely, "quit messing around and tell us what's been happening to you. How'd you get here, and what's going on?"

"Stowed away on *L'Olivino*," Joe said through a mouthful of bread. "It was kind of an accident—the ship took off while I was snooping around below. Dropped my phone in the water while I was sneaking aboard, so I couldn't call you."

I nodded. That was what I'd figured—well, at least, what I'd hoped.

"So what did you find out?" Nancy asked him. "Is this island the home base for a violent Corsican separatist group?"

Joe swallowed. "I don't know how you figured that out, but yes, it is," he said. "And you'll never guess who's leading them."

"Joanna Paoli," I supplied. He stared at me. I grinned. "We've got our own sources," I told him.

"Is Claude Bonaire involved with the separatists?" Nancy asked.

"Bonaire?" Joe looked baffled. "Not that I know of. Why would he be?"

"He happens to own this island," I explained. "I found out yesterday. That's how we knew about this place at all. He's building a replica of Claudius's Emerald Bower here."

Joe let out a long whistle. "No kidding. Well, that explains a lot." He polished off the last of the croissant and tossed the empty bag back into the boat. "Come on, you guys. Follow me. I've got some things to show you."

Caitlin was still looking weak and bedraggled, so we decided she should stay with the boat. I showed her how to start it so that if anyone came, she could make a quick retreat. "I hope I don't have to," she said, her voice tremulous.

"Me too," I said. "I'd rather not be stranded here!"

Then Joe led us into the trees, charting a course up a steep, heavily forested hill. Nancy followed him, and I brought up the rear.

Five or ten minutes of stiff climbing brought us to the top of the hill, where we paused to rest and catch our breath.

"We need to keep the noise down from here on," Joe cautioned in a low voice. "The separatist camp is at the north end of the island, but it's a small island."

"Got it," Nancy and I said together. We followed Joe north through the woods, keeping a sharp eye out for stray separatists. After about half an hour, we came to a spot where the land sloped up to a clifflike drop-off. Joe signaled for us to get down. Then he dropped to his belly and crawled like a soldier the last few yards to the edge.

I wriggled up on one side of him, and Nancy came up on the other. We found ourselves looking down on a construction site. On the left was the almost-finished building that had to be Bonaire's Emerald Bower. Palettes of marble slabs and red roof tiles sat beside it. On the right was a cluster of prefab huts, with one set well apart from the others.

"I was up here scoping out the scene when I saw your boat out there," Joe whispered. "I had my binocs with me, so I could tell it was you guys. I'm pretty sure no one else saw you—they were all sleeping. Let's hope they still are. They had a celebration last night that went pretty late."

"What were they celebrating?" Nancy asked.

Joe's eyes were somber. "That's what I'm about to show you."

"Wait a sec," I said. "Give me the binoculars, Joe."

He passed me the field binocs and I aimed them at the unfinished house. Aha! Just as I'd suspected.

"See those two statues in the front area?" I said, pointing. "The small ones that look like Pekingese dogs?"

"Yeah, so?" Joe replied.

I handed the binoculars back to him. "Unless I miss my guess, those are the missing Emerald-Eyed Lions."

"You've got to be kidding," Nancy said. "You mean the separatists are also the dig thieves?"

"I'm not sure," I said. "But my guess is that Bonaire really wanted those lions, and Joanna offered to get them for him. And now she has a hold over him, which she uses to keep him quiet and out of her way."

"Smart," Nancy said admiringly.

"That's my brother, always thinking," Joe said, grinning at me. Then his smile faded. "But right now we've got bigger fish to fry. Follow me."

We crept down the hill toward the isolated prefab hut, taking the utmost care not to make any sound. Joe scuttled across to the door, checked to see that no one was looking, and then threw it open. I could see that a broken padlock hung from the hasp.

Joe pointed silently into the dark interior. Nancy and I stepped in and Joe followed, closing the door behind us. The hut was in deep shadow, but I could see that it was piled high with wooden crates. The top was off one and the butt of a semiautomatic rifle poked out from a nest of straw.

"Weapons cache," Nancy whispered. "Whoa."

"That's not all," Joe said. He pointed to a medium-size case, made of silvery metal, that stood by itself.

"What's that?" I asked, though I had a sinking feeling that I already knew the answer.

Joe knelt and opened the lid. Nancy and I found ourselves gazing down at a dull gray metal sphere, roughly the size of a soccer ball. It was nestled in a bed of foam.

"Is that what I think it is?" Nancy's voice shook a little.

I nodded, hardly believing it myself. "It's a plutonium detonator. Wow. Oh, wow."

A plutonium detonator could mean only one thing.

The separatists were making a nuclear bomb!

JOE

"That's right," I said, nodding. "It came in on the *Olivino* last night. I saw them bring it aboard. I checked it out last night while they were all partying and my Geiger counter went nuts." I pulled it out and it began to make a loud chattering sound.

Frank snapped his fingers. "Hey, that's what that noise must have been in the warehouse that day. Right before the dogs attacked me I heard a noise just like that, only much fainter. I couldn't figure out what it was, but I had my Geiger counter in my backpack. It must have sensed the plutonium."

"So that's why they were celebrating," Nancy said. "It must have been hard—and expensive—to get ahold of this thing!"

"I wonder if they're really planning to use it," Frank mused. "Or is it just a blackmail tool?"

"Does it matter?" I replied, irked. Sometimes Frank is just too detached. "Either way, seems to me there's only one thing for us to do. We've got to get this detonator off the island and hand it over to the Italian government."

"You mean—carry it off ourselves?" Nancy's blue eyes widened. "I've never handled one of these things. What if we accidentally set it off?"

"We won't," Frank assured her. He gave a humorless smile. "I've never handled one either—I doubt many people outside the weapons business have—but I've read plenty about them. You need a powerful conventional explosive to trigger this baby, and that's always stored separately until the bomb is ready to be activated."

"Hey, not to rush you two or anything," I said, "but time's a-wasting here. The Corsicans aren't going to sleep forever. Can we go already?"

Frank and Nancy exchanged glances. Then Frank nodded. "Let's do it."

I took the carry handle at the front end of the case, and Frank took the back. The thing was surprisingly heavy—probably about fifty pounds in all. We hefted it and waited while Nancy opened the door. Then we headed out into the sunshine.

Where I stopped short. Because, facing us with a dumbfounded look on her face, was Joanna Paoli.

But the blank look didn't last long. Before I could even set the case down, Joanna had reached behind her and pulled an ugly-looking automatic pistol from her waistband. She pointed it at me.

"Don't move," she said softly.

RUN FOR IT!

The sudden stillness outside warned me that something was wrong. Then I heard a female voice saying, "Don't move."

I peeked out from the hut. My heart skipped a beat as I saw a young woman with long black hair and green eyes facing Joe and Frank. She was aiming a gun at Joe, and from the way she held it I was certain she knew how to use it.

I saw her take a deep breath and open her mouth, and I realized she was about to call for backup. I couldn't let that happen. There wasn't time to think. I just grabbed the padlock that was dangling from the hasp of the door, took aim, and threw.

Whap! It struck her square in the middle of her

forehead. Her green eyes opened wide with surprise.

Then the gun fell from her hand and she keeled over backward.

I let out the breath I hadn't known I'd been holding. Hurrying outside, I knelt by her and made sure she was breathing. She was, though there was a large egg-shaped lump rising on her forehead already. That was going to hurt later on.

I touched the bruise on my own head. *Payback*, I thought with a measure of satisfaction.

I turned around—and saw Frank and Joe staring at me with identical expressions of idiotic shock, their mouths hanging open.

"Well, don't just stand there," I said in an urgent whisper. "Help me get her into the shed before she wakes up!"

That woke them up. Setting down the case that held the detonator, the boys grabbed the woman—who I guessed was Joanna Paoli, the leader of the Corsican separatists—by her arms and legs and heaved her inside the hut. Frank pulled the door closed and stuck the broken padlock on the hasp to keep it shut. "That ought to buy us a couple of minutes," he muttered.

"Good. Now let's get out of here!"

As I led the way back up the slope, Joe said, "Nancy, with an arm like that you should be pitching in the major leagues!"

"Seriously," Frank agreed. "That was amazing!"

"It was just luck," I said, but I felt a warm glow in my cheeks.

"Yeah, sure. Just remind me to be on your team if we ever play softball," Joe said.

We hurried over the crest of the cliff and into the forest. On this trip we weren't worrying much about keeping the noise down. We were trying to go fast. It was tough, though, for the Hardy brothers. The case was heavy, and even with the carry handles it was an awkward burden on the uneven terrain. I winced as I saw how they were struggling.

Behind us, shots rang out. We heard confused yelling, and then a woman's voice rose over the babble, shouting commands.

"She got out. They're onto us!" Frank rasped.

We gave up any hope of keeping quiet and just ran. I went in the lead, seeking out the easiest footing for the boys.

It was a nightmare run. Branches slapped my face and thorny bushes ripped at my clothes as I plunged through the woods. Behind me, I heard Frank and Joe gasping and stumbling. And behind *them* I could hear the voices of the separatists, growing closer—fast.

Then we were sliding down the cliff that led to the cove where we'd left Caitlin and the boat.

"Caitlin!" I screamed. "Start the engine! Start it up!"

For a moment I heard nothing. Then the engine sputtered—and died. And again. And again.

"She flooded it," Frank gasped. "Tell her—stop!"

"Caitlin, stop!" I yelled. "Don't touch anything!"

We burst out onto the beach and I caught a glimpse of Caitlin's terrified face peeking over the side of the boat. I threw myself down by the boulder where I'd tied the painter rope and began feverishly undoing the knot.

The Corsicans were close behind us now—I could see flashes of movement among the trees as they began descending the cliff. Frank and Joe splashed through the shallow water to the boat and heaved the carry case over the side. Then Joe vaulted in and ran to the controls.

I've never heard a sweeter sound than that engine roaring to life. Pulling apart the last loop of the knot, I gathered the rope in my hands and raced to the boat. Frank and Caitlin hauled me over the side even as Joe was spinning the nose around.

"Watch out for the rocks!" Frank yelled.

"Got it!" Joe yelled back. He steered for the narrow opening.

The first of the separatist soldiers crashed onto the beach. I gasped. It was the guy who'd attacked me yesterday! As he spotted me, his face twisted in a snarl. He lowered his gun and took aim. I knew I should duck, but I couldn't seem to move.

But I didn't have to. With Frank navigating, Joe had

steered the boat past the rocks. Now in the clear, he gunned the motor and we shot away so fast that I lost my balance and fell sprawling onto the deck. I'll never know if my attacker fired at me, because the only thing I could hear was the roar of the boat's powerful engine.

"Yes!" Joe shouted, punching the air with his fist.

"Are we safe?" Caitlin cried.

Frank grabbed my hand and pulled me up off the deck, and then we were hugging, laughing, and cheering as we watched the island recede into the distance behind us.

"We did it," I yelled. "We really did it!"

"Wow, Nancy, we can't leave you alone for a second," George teased me.

"Seriously. Speedboats . . . terrorists . . . nuclear bombs . . . I can't believe the amount of trouble you got into in less than twenty-four hours away from us!" Bess joined in.

"Hey, it wasn't *all* my fault," I protested. I nodded toward Joe and Frank, who were seated at the round table in the kitchen of our pensione. "These two characters had a lot to do with it."

Joe paused in the act of shoveling a huge forkful of Aunt Estelle's pasta Bolognese into his mouth. "Guilty," he mumbled.

"Not to mention Caitlin Boggs," George added. She

shook her head. "That girl is just a trouble magnet. I'm glad we were able to help her, but I have to say I'm also glad she's gone."

"Me too," Bess agreed. We'd said good-bye to Caitlin the evening before, when her father had arrived to take her home. From the way she described him I'd been expecting a monster, but he turned out to be a pleasant enough man, as far as I could tell. He seemed genuinely concerned about Caitlin. He told me that he'd tried to stay in touch with her over the years but that his ex-wife had denied him access to her. I hoped that, in time, Caitlin would find some security and peace with him.

All that came after our escape from the island, though. First, when we reached the mainland, we'd been met by a huge contingent of military police, thanks to the calls Frank had made from his cell on the way back from the island. They'd taken charge of the bomb detonator and then whisked us off to a nearby army base for debriefing. Simultaneously an air squad had been sent out to the separatists' island base, where they'd all been rounded up and their weapons stockpile seized. The only person they hadn't found was Joanna Paoli, the ringleader. Somehow she'd escaped.

Also seized were the two Emerald-Eyed Lion statues from Claude Bonaire's villa. Bonaire had been brought in for questioning, though it seemed unlikely that the

Italian government would press charges against him. His story was that Joanna Paoli must have stolen the statues without his knowledge, and since she hadn't been caught yet, there was no one to contradict him.

"What's going to happen with Sam Lewis now?" I asked Frank. "Did you ever get him to talk?"

Frank nodded. "Once he learned that Caitlin was safe, he was more than willing to tell us everything. His story pretty much fills in the holes in what she told us."

"That night in the warehouse, Sam was on his way out when he heard Caitlin screaming his name," Joe said, picking up the tale from Frank. "He ran back and saw that she was being held by a bunch of men with guns. He didn't know what to do—there was no way he could overpower them. He figured maybe they were kidnappers, so he sneaked away and grabbed the box of stuff Caitlin had set aside from the dig, figuring that if he could sell it online he might be able to come up with some ransom money."

"Ooookay," George said, raising an eyebrow. "A little harebrained maybe, but I guess the guy was under some serious pressure."

"The problem was, when he tried to sell the stuff, of course he got caught," Frank continued. "And that's when things really got complicated. Joanna Paoli realized he had been there that night, and that he knew something about her operation. She somehow got a message to him while he was in police custody, telling him that if he told the police anything, Caitlin would suffer."

"So that's why he wouldn't say anything. He was trying to protect Caitlin," I murmured, nodding. "Poor guy. He got sucked into this whole crazy case against his will. He's the least guilty of any of them, and now he's the one who'll have to pay for his crimes."

"Well, hopefully we'll be able to help out there," Joe said. "ATAC is doing what it can to get the charges against him dismissed." He leaned back in his chair. "That was the best Bolognese sauce I've ever tasted."

I laughed. "Aunt Estelle's cooking is definitely a highlight of being here. Honestly, though, this has been the most exciting trip I've ever taken!"

"Amnesiacs, terrorists, stolen artifacts, and all?" Frank teased.

I smiled around the table at my friends. "And all," I confirmed. "In fact, I wouldn't have it any other way!"